About the Author

Award-winning author Anthony Masters knows how 'to hook his reader from the first page' *Books for Keeps.*

Anthony has written extensively for young adults and is renowned for tackling serious issues through gripping stories. He also writes for adults, both fiction and non-fiction. For the Orchard Black Apple list he has written the *Ghosthunter* series, the *Dark Diaries* series and four novels: *Spinner, Wicked, The Drop* and *Day of the Dead*, which was shortlisted for the Angus Award. He lives in Sussex with his wife and has three children.

Anthony Masters also runs *Book Explosions*, children's adventure workshops that inspire adrenalin and confidence in children, so that they can do their own creative writing.

Also by Anthony Masters

Dark Diaries

DEAD RINGER
FIRE STARTER
DEATH DAY
SHOCK WAVES

DAY OF THE DEAD
WICKED
THE DROP

Ghosthunters

DANCING WITH THE DEAD
DARK TOWER
DEADLY GAMES

Predator

SHARK ATTACK
DEATHTRAP
KILLER INSTINCT

hunted

ANTHONY MASTERS

ORCHARD BOOKS

With thanks to my good friend Allard Rolls,
for his advice and expertise concerning the
skiing sequences and to my much loved son,
Simon, for his knowledge of survival.

ORCHARD BOOKS
96 Leonard Street, London EC2A 4XD
Orchard Books Australia
32/45-51 Huntley Street, Alexandria, NSW 2015
ISBN 1 84121 904 5
First published in Great Britain in 2003
A paperback original
Text © Anthony Masters 2003
The right of Anthony Masters to be identified as the author
of this work has been asserted by him in accordance with
the Copyright, Designs and Patents Act, 1988.
A CIP catalogue record for this book is available from
the British Library.
1 3 5 7 9 10 8 6 4 2
Printed in Great Britain

Contents

For Sarah Dudman

Panic

The electrical storm was getting worse and the four-seater Cessna shook, engines roaring against the full blast of the gale. Luke was terrified, certain that they would soon be forced down on to the snow-covered mountains below, a vast expanse of jagged peaks that now seemed horribly near.

Luke had just seen what he thought was an avalanche, as rocks and great banks of snow slid noiselessly down a gully. If the Cessna came down here they wouldn't stand a chance.

The light aircraft shuddered and Luke glanced across at his cousin Finn, who was sitting next to him, avoiding eye contact. Luke was sure he knew the reason why. Finn was determined not to show how afraid he was, and that had been the problem ever since the start of the trip. Finn wouldn't, couldn't show his feelings. He had to be perfect – brave and super-efficient and completely sure he was right. They had already had a couple of days' skiing, staying in a resort hotel, and Finn had been deliberately patronising about Luke's abilities.

"You're not as experienced as I thought," he'd told Luke more than once, sapping his confidence and making him feel clumsy and awkward.

Luke had tried to tolerate Finn's attitude because he knew how much he'd suffered, but it was hard not to feel put down.

Even his own father, Sam Taylor, seemed inferior to Finn's father Brett, who was a brilliant skier as well as an experienced pilot. The two men were brothers, but they couldn't have been more different. Brett, who was in his early forties, had emigrated to North America in his late teens and become a park ranger. Sam was Head of English at a South London comprehensive school.

Now they were all in Canada on a kind of holiday. Sam was in the co-pilot's seat while Brett was flying the plane, but even in this crisis Brett was talking almost casually to the flight controllers at Rock Airport, where he still expected to land, despite the extreme weather conditions.

Luke could just hear Control at Rock responding in what he thought was an alarmingly unhelpful way. "We advise you to divert. Repeat – we advise you to divert."

But Brett was insistent. "I'm low on fuel. I have to come in."

The flight controllers responded immediately, reversing their original decision. Their reply made Luke realise how serious the situation was. "OK. We have you on radar. We'll talk you down. We'll have emergency services standing by. Good luck."

A peak veered up out of the rapidly darkening gloom and Luke was certain they were going to crash. The Cessna was so close to the mountain he could see the snow-covered fir trees.

Brett's plan had always been to fly them to Rock, a

small airport in a broad mountain valley within easy access of the nature reserve where they could enjoy some cross-country skiing. All the gear was stowed in the hold in the tail of the Cessna, although their backpacks were stacked at the rear of the cabin.

Luke began to shake, his mouth dry. They wouldn't get any skiing now. They were going to die instead. Their bodies wouldn't be found and he'd never see Mum and his sister again. And as for— Luke brought himself up short, trying to force the raw panic out of his system. Brett was an experienced pilot, he told himself, and this was just a bad storm. The landing was going to be fine. After all, his own father didn't look particularly worried. Or did he? Luke could see his father's hands were clutching the arms of his seat so hard that his knuckles showed white.

Finn had begun whistling, although the tune was more like a dirge and could barely be heard above the engines and the screaming of the wind outside. The whistling was getting on Luke's nerves, but he said nothing.

Luke wished again that he could make some kind of contact with his cousin. But communication wasn't

Finn's strong point. Luke knew Finn had experienced something so awful last year that Luke couldn't even begin to imagine how he had coped.

Finn's little brother, Karl, had been dragged off a camp site during the night – not a million miles away from here, in fact – by a wolf. At least, that was what everyone had supposed, as, although there had been a trail of blood leading into the forest from Finn and Karl's tent, Karl's body had never been found. But Finn was convinced his brother was alive. This conviction had become an obsession.

"We'll find him one day," Finn had told Luke so many times he'd lost count. "Karl's a resourceful sort of kid. He'd be able to live in the wild."

Luke had nodded feebly, not daring to meet Finn's eyes, but he could feel the force of his obsession, as if Finn was saying over and over again inside his head: *You've got to believe me. You've got to believe me*.

Dad had told Luke that Finn had been through months of counselling yet he still clung fiercely to this impossible dream. The tragedy and its aftermath was the main reason why they had all met, and why they were flying through a storm in a light aircraft that now seemed as fragile as a moth.

To distract himself from the roaring of the Cessna's engines and the buffeting of the gale, Luke tried to focus on his cousin, attempting to work out how he could help him.

Finn was stockily built like his father, but there the similarity ended. Finn was competitive and aggressive, determined to prove himself better than Luke at everything. Not that that was particularly hard, Luke thought. From the moment they'd all met, Luke had felt right out of his depth – threatened by Finn's aggression, and all too conscious of his own skinny frame. Finn seemed much more able than he would ever be, despite the fact that he'd been so traumatised by the appalling death of his younger brother.

Dad had tried to talk to Luke about his cousin before they left London.

"I want you to enjoy the trip, but I'm also hoping you'll help Finn come to grips with his life. You know what happened. But he's got this fantasy that Karl could still be alive."

"And being brought up by a wolf pack?" Luke had asked curiously, wondering for a moment if that was possible. Just after Karl's disappearance, the press had had a field day, even in the British newspapers. He could remember the headlines now:

```
BOY ABDUCTED BY WOLVES IN CANADA
COULD KARL TAYLOR STILL BE ALIVE?
TRAIL OF BLOOD MAKES HOPES FADE
```

The possibility that Karl might still be alive, or at least, the rumours put about by the hysterical media, had clearly fuelled the grief-stricken Finn's hopes. But his parents didn't share Finn's obsession.

Luke dimly remembered reading years ago about the discovery of a wolf boy who had been brought up by the pack since he was snatched as a young child – and who had learned to run on all fours with the wolves. Luke had been intrigued, but his Dad was openly dismissive. The idea of a wolf boy running with the pack in a forest was too far away from the urban reality of his comprehensive school in Balham to hold any credibility.

"Finn was very close to Karl – and he just hasn't been able to come to terms with his death," he had told Luke. "We *all* need to help him."

*

The aircraft gave a violent lurch as a flash of lightning lit up the mountains. Luke could see the rugged ice-bound peaks and the snow-covered tree-line further down the slopes. In the strange and unsettling grey light, the peaks looked close – far too close.

As his father wrestled with the controls even Finn seemed to be getting edgy. His whistling abruptly stopped.

"This flight's a bit bumpy," Finn said, trying to sound casual, but his shaky voice betrayed his unease.

Luke, however, was determined to give nothing away, despite the nausea that was welling up inside him. This was awful. He *couldn't* throw up. Finn would utterly despise him – if he didn't already.

"There are wolves down there!" Finn suddenly yelled as the Cessna banked across the valley.

"Shut up, Finn," Brett said absently, while he struggled for control as turbulence lifted the aircraft again. "I'm going to increase height. Maybe we can get above this weather."

As he eased up the nose of the Cessna, Brett suddenly seemed less professional, less in control and

Luke began to feel as if he had a fever, one minute boiling hot and sweating and the next freezing cold. He was more afraid now than he had ever been in his life.

Luke glanced across at Finn and was guiltily pleased to see the sweat on his forehead. I'm not alone, he thought, and then another anxiety filled him.

There are wolves down there, Luke heard Finn say over and over again in his mind. *There are wolves down there*. The only wolf Luke had ever seen had been safely behind bars in a zoo, and he could hardly remember what it looked like. But there was something about the word 'wolf' which conjured up a fearsome image of the animal. He could imagine their fangs and foul breath as they prowled towards him through the snow…

Luke desperately tried to control his panic, focusing on the back of his father's head.

"How are you doing, Dad?" Luke yelled.

"I'm fine. We'll be OK." His attempt at reassurance was so stilted it was deeply painful.

The Cessna was still climbing, lurching through the turbulence.

"How's the fuel?" asked Finn, uncharacteristically revealing his anxieties.

"Not so good." Brett's voice was clipped.

"How long?"

"Half an hour. Maybe a bit more."

"We got enough to make Rock?"

"Sure."

Another flash of lightning lit up the mountain range, making it look like a photographic negative. Thunder boomed and Luke saw blue flames shooting from the right-hand engine of the Cessna.

"More lightning?" Luke shouted, sure they were now in even greater trouble.

Brett's reply was lost.

"What?"

"We're losing fuel and we have ourselves a fire." Brett sounded incredulous, as if he couldn't believe what was happening.

"What do we do?" Sam was all too obviously trying not to sound anxious.

"We're an engine down, but we can fly on the other one and still make Rock." Brett seemed more confident now and Luke felt a surge of hope as the Cessna became more stable. Was Brett just trying to reassure them, or was their situation less dangerous than he had imagined? Conscious of being watched, Luke turned to Finn, but the naked fear he saw in his cousin's eyes destroyed Luke's optimism immediately.

"You OK?" Finn was still trying to sound laid-back and casual.

"Yes," said Luke, as the panic surged.

"We can hack it," said Sam. He turned round and grinned at the two boys, trying to show a confidence he didn't possess.

Luke felt ashamed and then disloyal. Dad sounded like some ancient Scoutmaster talking about an adventure, all jolly and hopeful, determined to hide his real feelings.

Then a grinding sound penetrated the aircraft cabin.

"What's that?" snapped Finn.

"The other engine," said Brett.

Luke watched his dad leaning towards his brother in disbelief. Then the remaining engine cut out and all he could hear was the banshee shriek of the gale.

*

Luke choked back a cry of despair. Would death hurt, he wondered. Or would he black out and feel nothing? But suppose he was the only survivor? Suppose he was condemned to wander the snow-bound wilderness alone?

He'd rather die than do that.

Crash

"I'm going to try and put her down," shouted Brett. "There's a valley down there without too many trees."

"Which valley?" Sam simply sounded curious, and Luke felt a surge of pride at his father's apparent calm.

"Down there," said Brett bleakly, his hands steady on the controls, but all Luke could see were the jagged peaks, half lost to sight in snow flurries. To his relief, a strange numbness had replaced the panic and fear, but part of him wondered if that was acceptance – an acceptance that they were all going to die.

"Can – can we make it?" asked Finn hesitantly.

"Sure." Brett sounded as reassuring as Finn obviously wanted him to be.

Suddenly the Cessna began to drop and Luke watched the snow flurries increase until all he could see was whiteness, with the occasional glimpse of rock and pine trees. He stared out, as detached as if he was watching a film. Then, suddenly, the Cessna began to shake and all Luke's fears returned, sweat breaking out all over his body.

"Hang on, son. We'll make it," shouted Dad.

Now the cabin windows were covered in snow and ice and Luke couldn't see out at all. He felt as if he was in a flying coffin.

Then the Cessna juddered and went nose down.

For a moment nothing happened, as if time was suspended, and Luke had a mental image of the grandfather clock at home with its hands stuck and its usually loud ticking silent. Then panic took over as the plane hit something hard and Luke felt he was being pressed down by a huge weight. A backpack shot forward from behind his seat and hit him hard round the shoulders.

The lights went out as the Cessna careered on with a metallic screaming, sliding down a slope. Luke could just see Dad and Uncle Brett ducking down as the windscreen smashed and a blast of freezing cold air surged into the cabin. Then he was thumped in the chest so forcefully that all the wind was knocked out of him. He could just see part of Dad's seat had broken loose.

As Luke gasped for breath he realised the Cessna was now sliding at considerable speed, cutting through trees, the metallic roar getting louder and louder. Part of the fuselage had been torn open and for a moment Luke thought he was going to be hurled out of the plane. He just managed to save himself. Clinging frantically to the back of his father's seat, Luke could see himself falling down the mountainside, hitting trees as the plane sliced through them.

Banks of snow hurtled past, the Cessna swung round and there was a sharp impact which at last brought the plane to a clanking, grinding halt. Then there was silence, broken only by the raging of the wind.

Luke ached all over as he gazed up at the black night sky through a hole in the fuselage. He felt completely disorientated.

Then Luke heard a low moaning noise and a voice, high and shrill, saying over and over again, "Is that you, Dad? Are you all right, Dad?" It took some time to recognise it as his own.

The dreadful moaning sound continued, like an animal in pain.

"Are you OK, Dad?" asked Luke again.

"My leg – I can't move it." Sam's voice was hoarse with pain. But at least he could speak. "And I'm worried about Brett." The low moaning continued, sounding like a frightened animal.

"What's the matter with Dad?" asked Finn, his voice wobbling. He seemed to have been thrown out of his seat, despite his safety belt, and was picking himself up from somewhere at the back of the cabin.

"He needs some help." Sam sounded weak and apprehensive.

Luke dragged himself out of his own buckled seat, surprised to find he could stand, while Finn followed him.

"We need a torch." Luke could hardly speak as waves of shock hit him, making his heart pound.

"They're in the flight bag behind Dad's seat," gasped Finn.

Luke had a real struggle to recognise where anything was. The impact seemed to have contracted the layout of the cabin. Eventually he managed to locate the flight bag and after a frantic search he found he was at last grasping a torch.

Sweeping the cabin with the beam, all Luke could see was crumpled metal. The freezing wind tore at him through the gaping holes in the fuselage and he felt incredibly cold. Then he made contact with Finn's shoulder which was running with some kind of liquid. The smell of aviation fuel was so strong that for a crazy moment Luke wondered if the stuff was dripping from Finn.

"Stop pawing at me!" Finn snarled, pushing him away.

"What's this on your shoulder?"

"Blood. Why don't you try using the torch?"

Feeling incredibly stupid, Luke shone the beam over Finn only to see the blood streaming down his cousin's face.

"See if you can find something to mop it up." Finn's voice suddenly sounded thin, as if his aggression had drained away at the sight of his own blood.

Luke dragged out a filthy handkerchief from his pocket and mopped ineffectively at Finn's forehead.

Finn winced. "Give me that," he said impatiently.

Luke did so, then flashed the beam of the torch towards the cockpit, starting to edge his way through the compacted wreckage. He could still hear the low moaning sound, which was softer now.

As Luke flashed the torch around the shattered cockpit, he realised the damage to the plane was even worse than he'd imagined. Inside, the control panels were smashed and there was no lighting.

"What about the radio?" asked Luke. "Can't we send out an SOS?"

"No way," his dad's voice whispered from the darkness. "The radio's smashed – like everything else. We can't communicate with anyone."

Luke reached his father, sweeping both him and Brett with the beam. His dad had a few cuts and his leg was buckled under him. Brett, however, was unconscious and his breathing laboured. He was still making the low moaning sound.

"Brett," Luke whispered. There was no obvious sign of any major injury and Brett didn't seem to be losing any blood.

"For Christ's sake," called out Finn. "How's my father?"

"He's unconscious – but he's breathing."

"I can't move," muttered Sam, "and I've got a terrible headache."

Luke tried to help his dad shift his weight off the trapped leg and eventually Sam was able to straighten up a bit. But although his leg didn't seem to be broken, it was obviously giving him a lot of pain.

"We need to go for help." Finn's words tumbled over each other. "Maybe I can get the skis and sticks out of what's left of the hold. We've got protective clothing and if we start at first light we'll soon get to Rock. And anyway, they'll send a rescue party out for us – they must have seen us disappear from the radar." He sounded glib and overconfident.

"How far's Rock?" Luke asked tentatively.

"I don't know this mountain. Maybe Rock's in the

next valley. The air map should give us some idea – but it's nowhere near as good as a real one."

Luke tried to pull himself together. It all sounded so incredible, but what else could they do?

"Can't you hack it?" Finn suddenly demanded, making Luke feel like a wimp.

"Of course I can," Luke snapped. "What about the cut on your head?"

"It's fine," said Finn dismissively. "What's the time? My watch got broken in the crash."

"Just after ten." A new urgency overcame Luke. "Do we have to wait till morning?"

"Of course we have to wait. We wouldn't stand a chance in the dark," said Finn scornfully.

"How are we going to work out which way to go?"

"The air map and compass should be in this flight bag."

As Finn checked the bag, Luke swept Brett's grey features with his torch. His lips were moving and the moaning was much fainter.

"We're going for help in the morning, Dad. Finn reckons we can make it to Rock."

"Yeah." Sam sounded as if he hadn't really heard.

"We'll soon get help." Luke's words seemed to hang in the freezing cold air, trite and stupid.

"How are you going to find Rock?" Sam's voice was muzzy and weak.

"Finn knows the way."

Sam Taylor seemed to regain some clarity. "Remember our map reading? When we were up in the Cairngorms?"

"Yes." Luke hoped Finn had more experience than that.

"Look after Finn," said his father as if suddenly reading Luke's thoughts. He spoke in a whisper. "He's not been well since Karl. You know that."

You can say that again, thought Luke. He was about to go out into a snow-covered, hostile landscape and try to ski to Rock, which might or might not be in the next valley, with someone who believed his brother was still alive, someone who wasn't even stable. But what was the alternative?

Then he heard howling in the distance and felt the hairs prickling on the back of his neck. "What's that?"

"A wolf," said Finn.

*

Luke watched snowflakes beginning to swirl and thicken through the gaping hole in the side of the Cessna. At that moment, Finn shoved the bloodied handkerchief into the pocket of his jeans, grabbed the torch from Luke and jumped out into the snow.

"Where're you going?" called Luke, his fear of isolation returning.

"I'm going to try and open the rear hold."

Luke waited anxiously in the dark. His cousin seemed to be taking an incredibly long time. Several times Luke called out, but there was no reply.

Then Finn suddenly appeared at the hole, holding the strap of the torch between his teeth and grappling with cross-country skis and sticks. Having passed them up to Luke, he disappeared, soon returning with two skisuits with hoods, skins, boots and crampons. Scrambling back into the Cessna, he swore at Luke for getting in the way, making him feel even more inadequate. As Finn pushed past him, Luke saw that the flow of blood from the wound on his cousin's forehead seemed to have dried up.

"Get out of the way," Finn rasped again. "You're making things worse."

Luke didn't think he was, but this was no time to argue. He rummaged around in the space behind Brett's seat and dragged out a square object that turned out to be the first-aid box with a second torch in it. "Shall I put something over that cut?"

"I'm OK," snapped Finn.

"It could start bleeding again."

"I don't care. Can't you see I'm more worried about my father?" Finn scowled at him.

There was a silence.

Then Finn snarled, "Do your first-aid stuff then."

Luke got a plaster out of the first-aid box which he stuck over the cut on Finn's forehead. Then, with a display of determined independence, Luke began preparing their kit for the next day. He grabbed two rucksacks, shoving in some of the food they had brought with them, largely chocolate and sandwiches, fruit, a few soft drinks and a couple of bottles of water. After rummaging around in the wreck of the cabin he found a box of emergency supplies, including some hot cans which, as Brett had already told them, were specially designed with a self-heating device. He also added ski gloves and socks as well as the compass and the map.

Luke felt better as he worked, surprised and gratified by his own unexpected resourcefulness. He hoped Finn would be impressed, but he was busy checking out the cross-country skis he had brought in from the hold. They were longer and narrower than downhill skis and Luke had little experience of them. He and Dad had spent a couple of days using them in Norway, but that seemed a long time ago.

Finn then added some of the first-aid kit to the rucksack but only after carefully checking what had already been packed, making Luke feel useless again, his new-found confidence destroyed.

"I hope you're going to keep up," said Finn. "You're not anything like as experienced as I am."

"So maybe you'd better go alone," replied Luke bitterly.

"You scared?" Finn was staring at him, with a strange look in his eyes that Luke didn't recognise. Could it be concern?

"I was just wondering…" Luke suddenly wanted to provoke Finn. "Do you *really* know what you're doing?"

"Of course I do." Finn was full of contempt.

"Shut up, you two," interrupted Sam's voice from the crushed cockpit. "If you start arguing now, you won't stand a chance. We're depending on you both to make it to Rock. Got it?"

Finn and Luke eyed each other. Luke knew it was true.

"You really reckon you know the way, Finn?" asked Sam.

"Yeah. We'll be OK."

"And the wolves?" asked Luke uncertainly.

"I told you—"

"*Are* there wolves?" Sam's voice was weakening.

Finn brushed past Luke, heading for the crumpled figure of his father who was breathing raggedly. Luke was surprised he hadn't checked him out before, or maybe he hadn't dared. His spirits rose a little. At last his cousin was showing a few chinks in his armour-plated confidence.

Finn grabbed his father's wrist. "Dad, we're going for help in the morning. We're going to get to Rock. So, you've got to be here when we get back. Can you hear me, Dad?" Finn's last question sounded panicky.

"Of course he can hear you," said Sam encouragingly, but Luke wondered how long Brett could last without medical help.

Finn glanced at Sam suspiciously. "How do you know that?" But he didn't wait for an answer and turning back to Luke, he snapped, "Let's try and get some sleep."

The Young Wolf

The howling woke Luke in the
night and for a moment he had absolutely no idea
where he was. Then the horror of the crash
returned.

Slowly and blearily he got to his feet and limped
towards a hole in the fuselage.

Then he saw them, lit by the pale light of a
crescent moon.

There were about half a dozen wolves, their bodies
much bigger and broader than a dog's, legs long and

sinewy with huge paws. They were in a semicircle, staring at the wrecked plane, their eyes fixed on his own. Some were crouching, others standing, grey fur quivering.

Then Finn woke. "What's happening?"

But Luke didn't reply. He couldn't.

Light snow began to fall and one of the wolves howled, another joining in on a different note, and then yet another. Soon all the wolves were howling, and the sounds they made became a song. Luke listened to the eerie, haunting sound.

Then, as if at a given signal, the song abruptly ceased and the wolves padded away into the trees.

"That was incredible," whispered Luke to himself as relief flooded through him.

"They're amazing," Finn said quietly. "That's how they talk to each other – by howling. And those wolves jog along at twenty-five miles an hour, but they can reach speeds of forty when they go in for a kill." He sounded reverent, as if he was describing something that was darkly magical. "They can leap right up in the air and can jump like cats." Finn paused. "And they can dance too. I bet Karl dances with them."

Luke felt a jolt of dismay. Had Finn gone crazy? Luke decided to play safe. "You've studied them?"

"You bet I have." Finn stared at Luke, his expression hard to read. "They can smell their prey up to a kilometre away. Maybe more. They've got excellent hearing too – they can hear high frequency sounds. And they can see in the dark too." Finn was gabbling out the words now. Then he seemed to pull himself together. "OK, let's try and get back to sleep. Tomorrow's going to be tough."

Luke tried unsuccessfully to push away his mounting fears. Now they had a wolf pack snapping at their heels. Surely they would be hungry in this snow-bound wilderness? Luke visualised the dark creatures following him and Finn as they trekked through the snow. Choosing their moment, they sprang, ready to make the perfect kill.

"They've got forty-two huge teeth," said Finn, back to his gabbling voice, as if reading from a textbook. "Their fangs can slash and crack their way through bone and muscle."

There was a long silence, eventually broken by Luke. "Where did you get all this from?" he asked uncomfortably.

"I know wolves. I need to know about them. For Karl." He paused, and then continued. "They wouldn't have harmed Karl. They wouldn't hurt a kid."

"No?" asked Luke doubtfully. This was madness, he thought. Absolute madness.

"No," replied Finn. He suddenly grabbed Luke's neck in a strong grip and squeezed painfully.

"Get off!" yelled Luke.

"They don't usually attack humans anyway. They're simply curious. And they certainly wouldn't hurt a kid. Not a kid as young as Karl." Finn's voice died away and his grip on Luke's neck slackened.

Was Finn still in shock? Luke shivered in the cold, dreading what the next day might bring.

Luke couldn't sleep, hunched up in what was left of his seat, listening to his father snoring, Brett groaning occasionally and heavy breathing from Finn. But eventually he dozed off, dreaming of a young boy running lithely on all fours among a pack of wolves. He woke abruptly. A strange smell filled his nostrils, and he half sat up in his seat.

A young wolf had jumped in through a hole in the fuselage and the rank smell was becoming stronger by the second.

"Don't move," hissed Finn. "It's only curious."

Luke froze, mesmerised by the eyes that seemed fixed on his own in the darkness.

The wolf was snuffling round one of the rucksacks.

Then there came a muted growl from outside and the wolf froze, listening, ears pricked. Luke knew he couldn't contain himself much longer. He had to shout, to warn Dad and Brett, to—

The young wolf turned, listened again and then leapt back out through the hole in the fuselage.

The pungent smell faded and there was a long silence.

Survival

Luke slept dreamlessly and a few hours later woke in dim dawn light. He glanced round, suddenly remembering how a wolf had invaded the cabin. How could Finn think that his brother now lived with animals like these? In the freezing cold cabin, Finn's belief seemed terrifying. Was he mad, or deluded, or both? Right now, however, there was no sign of him.

Luke stumbled to his feet, feeling guilty at having overslept and even guiltier about being ravenously hungry. Why hadn't he thought about Dad or Brett yesterday? They'd need warmth and food, quickly. Had he been in complete shock?

He leant between the pilots' seats and called huskily, "Dad?"

"Yes?" His father sounded reassuringly alert.

"How do you feel?"

"My leg hurts, but the rest of me seems OK."

"Do you want something to eat?"

"Finn brought me a couple of sandwiches and a bar of chocolate." Luke felt glad that his dad had had some food, but annoyed that his cousin had beaten him to the initiative. He also noticed that their fathers were both warmly wrapped in sleeping bags, which had been unzipped to act like blankets, and felt ashamed that he hadn't thought of it himself.

"What about drink?"

"There's a bottle of water here. I've even managed to get some down Brett."

"You mean he's conscious?" Luke was amazed.

"Did you think I was dead?" Brett suddenly whispered.

"No, of course not," said Luke hurriedly. Maybe things weren't going to be so bad after all. "Where do you hurt?" he asked.

"All over."

Some of Luke's optimism faded.

"Where's Finn?" Luke wondered if his cousin had decided to make the expedition on his own.

"Gone for a recce," said Sam.

"Finn knows what he's doing." Brett winced and Luke was sure that despite his return to consciousness, Brett was in a lot of pain. "Rock can't be that far. Maybe ten or fifteen miles – something like that," he added vaguely.

"Save your strength, Brett," Sam advised him. "We're going to be all right. Take some more food, Luke – there's more sandwiches in my bag. We've got enough. Finn has given us a stack of hot tins of food too. Don't forget to take the rest with you."

Luke shivered. He had been so exhausted that he hadn't felt the cold during the night. But now he was really feeling the freezing temperature.

He wrenched his father's bag from behind the seats and found some cake which tasted utterly delicious. He then took several swigs from the bottle of water, only to find he had been so preoccupied that he hadn't even heard Finn clambering back into the plane.

"Pigging out?" Finn's remark made Luke jump guiltily.

"Do you want some?" asked Luke, looking down at the crumbs in the box.

"There doesn't seem to be much left." Finn grinned.

"Sorry," Luke replied uneasily.

"Don't worry. I had one of the sandwiches you put in our backpacks." Finn's grin widened as he noticed Luke's discomfort, but he didn't seem unfriendly or his usual mocking self. "You ready. We should get going." He paused. "I've checked out the route on the air map and have also packed one of the torches and a light-weight tent. Just in case."

"In case of what?"

"That Rock's further away than I think."

There was a silence.

Then Luke said, "I'll get kitted up."

"Do that." Finn was brisk as he leant over his father. "How are you, Dad?"

Brett's whisper was thinner than ever. "I'll be waiting for you."

"You'd better be." Finn was commanding. Then he

turned back to Luke. "What are you hanging about for?" he snarled.

Sam reached out a hand and gripped Luke's wrist. "Keep safe," he said. "I'm sure my leg's not broken. As long as I take it slowly I'll be able to move about and look after Brett." He pulled Luke closer. "Don't worry about wolves. They're shy animals really." He paused. "Attacks are rare." His voice faltered and Luke could see tears in Sam's eyes. Were they tears of pain – or grief? Maybe they were both. "I'm proud of you," he whispered.

Luke nodded. "We'll get help," he said, shivering, but not just from the cold. "Don't worry."

"Come on." Finn was impatient. "We need to get going."

Once Luke was kitted up in his skisuit he felt warmer and much more purposeful. As he jumped out of the hole in the fuselage, pulled on his skis and picked up his sticks, he saw large paw prints in the snow. They were bigger than his hand.

"Just to prove you weren't dreaming," said Finn.

Luke turned to gaze down the long slope where the

prints disappeared into a dark line of trees. There were scars in the snow that marked the Cessna's crash landing, the deep furrows slewing as the plane hit trees on either side. Some had fallen.

The Cessna had finally come to rest against a large pine and the wreckage was strewn with pine needles and branches. A wing had broken off and the fuselage of the Cessna had been twisted by the force of the impact. They were amazingly lucky to be alive.

Luke gazed at Finn who was also staring at the tangled mess of metal. The tail was half buried in the snow that had fallen during the night and if any more fell the Cessna would be covered completely. But the site of the crash would still be recognisable by the fallen trees and splintered wood.

"I wonder if they've sent a search party yet," said Luke.

"Flying conditions are lousy." Finn was dismissive. "They'll be grounded until the weather improves."

"Can't we try and plug the holes in the fuselage with something – just in case the wolves come back?"

"Good thinking. It'll stop the snow drifting in, too. I reckon we could stuff them with some of the broken pine branches." Finn was suddenly talking to Luke as an equal and Luke felt more confident as they began to work.

After about half an hour they had managed to fill the gaps.

Then Finn yelled into the cabin, "We're going now. Take care."

Only Sam replied. "You do the same."

"How's Dad?" asked Finn suspiciously.

"He's fine," said Sam.

"We'll get help as soon as we can," said Luke.

"You do that." Luke thought his father suddenly sounded desperate.

The gale had blown itself out and there was a deep silence in the forest that was sinister and forbidding. The smell of aviation fuel was very strong.

"Is there any chance of fire?" asked Luke uneasily.

"No way," replied Finn, pulling on his bulky backpack which also contained the tent. He sounded as if he was trying to reassure himself.

Couldn't we have shared the load more, thought Luke. Was Finn still trying to prove something by taking on the extra weight? Maybe it was a habit – or he simply didn't think Luke could take the strain. Either way, the expedition seemed to be getting off to an unequal start. Then Luke remembered that Finn was a lot more experienced than he was and had probably made the right decision.

"There could be another snowstorm," said Finn, gazing up the valley which was overshadowed by a mountain peak laden with snow.

Trying to ignore Finn's pessimism, Luke shouldered his own backpack, which was a dead weight on his shoulders. He'd never carried such a heavy load before and, with his limited experience of cross-country skiing, he was worried about keeping up with Finn.

"Which way are we going?" he asked, noticing that his cousin had pulled out a pocket compass and was studying it carefully. Luke watched him uneasily, leaning on his sticks.

"We'll keep to the valley floor and head off through the forest. Maybe we'll find some kind of trail." Finn sounded uneasy as he pocketed the compass. "We need to head due west."

"How far?"

Finn shrugged. "If we ski hard then we might get to Rock by nightfall. If not, then we'll make a bivouac."

"What about the tent?"

"Depends if we're still in the forest. If we put up the tent inside a bivouac, we're going to be warmer." Finn was brisk, clearly not wanting to have to explain any more. Then he asked, "Do you reckon my dad's all right?"

Surprised, and unused to reassuring Finn, Luke said, "He sounded stronger."

"You're telling the truth?" For the first time, Luke felt Finn's anxiety.

Luke made a huge effort. "I'm telling you the truth."

Finn relaxed a little, seemingly at least temporarily satisfied.

As they skied away from the Cessna and into the forest the sun suddenly came out, making the snow sparkle. After a nerve-racking start when he was sure he was going to fall, Luke found the cross-country skiing much easier than he had thought, and he was able to keep up with Finn.

The pine forest was dark and gloomy, and deprived

of sunlight, except for the occasional beam that managed to filter through a group of thin saplings.

Soon the going became more difficult for Luke as Finn began to zig zag between the trees, just avoiding their trunks. Luke wasn't able to do the same and several times made contact, with painful results. Despite the hazards, Finn had barely slackened his speed and Luke was beginning to fall behind. Eventually, the all too familiar terror of being left alone overwhelmed him and Luke shouted, "You're going too fast!"

Finn stopped and returned to Luke reluctantly, with a scowl on his face. "You've got to keep up. This isn't a school trip."

Luke glanced at his watch. They'd only been going for an hour and already he felt completely exhausted.

"I'm trying to," he gasped, hardly able to draw enough breath to speak, gazing at the closely packed trees which seemed to go on for ever.

Finn's gaze softened and he suddenly smiled encouragingly at Luke. Was he making an effort, Luke wondered. "OK. I'll take the pace down a little." Finn paused. "Sorry, I should have realised."

"Realised what?" asked Luke defensively.

"I should have remembered you don't have my experience."

"So you think I'm letting you down?"

"No. I've just had a lot of practice out here, that's all. I don't suppose—" He broke off, gazing ahead.

Then Luke saw the wolf. It was about ten metres away, staring at them intently, ears laid flat, hair on end.

Slowly, Finn picked up a dead branch.

The wolf snarled and Luke tried to remain completely still as he watched his cousin slowly advance, the branch held high in his hand.

The wolf held its ground, lips drawn back in a snarl, and Luke could see its razor-sharp teeth.

Finn was much nearer the wolf now. Suppose the thing sprang up and ripped out his throat, thought Luke. He'd be at its mercy.

His hands shaking, Luke reached for another branch, and then realised the wood was rotten and would be of little use. Nevertheless, he joined Finn, standing in a sunbeam, motes of dust hazing around him.

The grey wolf shifted position, and then made a growling sound. Its tail was raised high in the air, back arched and tense.

Luke thought the creature was about to spring and more by instinct than anything else hurled the rotten branch, which only brushed the wolf's fur before falling into the snow and breaking in half.

The wolf paused, looking slightly surprised, and then continued to advance.

Finn threw down his sticks, wrenched off his skis, and gave an animalistic roar, but the wolf stood its ground. He roared again, hurling one of his skis which fell just short of the wolf's nose. Giving a sudden yelp of distress, it backed off and then turned away, running into the trees, swallowed up by the dense undergrowth.

"That was close," muttered Luke, the shock beginning to ripple through him.

Finn strode over to pick up his ski, staring into the trees.

"Do you think it'll come back with the rest of the pack?" asked Luke uneasily.

But Finn didn't reply, still gazing into the forest.

Luke couldn't forget those amber eyes, gleaming in the dull light of the pines. He imagined the powerful jaws driving the razor-sharp teeth through flesh and bone. *His* flesh and bone.

"What's the time?" asked Finn abruptly.

"Midday." The sun was high in the sky now, but the warmth was only fleeting.

"We'll stop soon and eat." Finn sounded friendly and Luke felt cheered, watching him pulling out two folded skins from his rucksack. "You have to use the skins over your skis for going uphill," said Finn. "Hook the tab over the front of each ski and then pull the skin over the blade. Like this." Finn hooked the folded piece of moleskin over one of his skis and stretched it out so that the sticky underside stuck to his ski. Then he did the same to the other one.

Luke clumsily tried to do the same, and then snapped open the catches behind the heels of his ski boots so that his feet were flexible for going uphill.

Following in his cousin's wake, Luke found he'd got a second wind and even his backpack seemed lighter as his skills grew. A surge of hope filled him. Surely they were getting nearer to Rock?

Luke's second encounter with a wolf had terrified him, but he still couldn't understand what Finn was feeling. He'd seen this wolf off, but another part of Finn was clearly fascinated by them, sure that his brother was now one of their number.

Now they were halfway up the hill and Luke was beginning to flag, his legs aching from the difficulty of walking uphill, despite the skins which helped the skis cling to the snow. Soon he began to fall back again, while the stockily built Finn pushed on without the slightest sign of exhaustion.

A burst of frustrated temper suddenly filled Luke and he glared at Finn's broad back with a rising hatred. The pain in Luke's legs was becoming unbearable and yet Finn showed no sign of stopping, even though the gap between them was widening and widening.

Suddenly Luke couldn't take any more. "Wait!" he yelled.

Finn didn't seem to hear and plodded on uphill. The ground was rising more sharply. The tree-line was thinning and they were heading for a rounded summit.

"Wait!" he yelled again.

Finn came to a halt. The sky had clouded over, light

snow was beginning to fall, and now they were more exposed, the cold was intense.

Finn waited for Luke to catch up with him. "What is it?" he asked impatiently.

"I'm knackered."

"We have to keep going."

Doubt suddenly filled Luke's heart. "Are we going in the right direction?"

"Rock should be in the next valley – but it's going to be a long climb and we'll have to take care skiing down – it's getting a lot steeper than I thought." He hesitated. "Look, I can't be absolutely sure, you know."

"Sure of what?" rapped out Luke.

"Whether Rock *is* in the next valley – or the one after that." Finn paused. "It's hard to use an air map on the ground, you know. It just shows the heights of the peaks and the depths of the valleys for the pilots. I think we may have to camp tonight."

Luke was shivering now, anxious to get more breath back. How high up were they, he wondered. The air seemed thin and he began to wonder if they would have enough oxygen to breathe. Suddenly he felt nausea turn in his stomach. "Can we take a break?" he pleaded, but Finn shook his head.

"We *have* to keep going," he repeated, patient but determined. "It'll be dark in a few hours."

"Do you think the wolves will come?"

"Not if we light a fire."

Luke was still so exhausted that he decided to try and gain a little more rest time by talking to Finn. "You don't really think Karl's still alive, living with the pack or something, do you?" Immediately, Luke felt ashamed, aware that he had gained time in the worst possible way.

There was a deep silence as the snowflakes thickened.

"I mean – they're wild animals," Luke blundered on.

"Shut up!" Finn's voice was steel.

"I'm only trying to—"

Finn advanced on him. "You shut your mouth."

Luke stared into his cousin's furious face, but before he could back down Finn had slapped him hard.

Luke gazed back at Finn, his cheek smarting. "Sorry," he mumbled, knowing he'd been stupid. Worse than stupid.

Finn turned away. "Let's move on. All you're doing is

wasting time, and if you can't keep up I'll leave you behind. My father's life is far more important than yours. Do you get it?"

Luke nodded. He'd never been so afraid but he got it all right.

Spray

Luke pushed on, the exhaustion still with him, made worse by his argument with Finn. Why couldn't he have understood how Finn had kept himself going, how he had kept his grief for his brother at bay.

Stumbling along, Luke recalled what his dad had told him about the disappearance of Karl. Because his body had never been recovered and because Finn had slept through the appalling attack, he had invented a protective fantasy that had helped him to cope. It was just his way of dealing with it.

Yet more shame filled Luke. Out here in this freezing wilderness, he had used desperate survival tactics, buying time by hurting Finn in the most insensitive way he could have chosen. As if they didn't have enough problems already.

As the light began to fade, the bitter cold seemed to penetrate Luke's very soul. So far there had been no mention of food and Luke wondered if Finn was trying to punish him.

When Luke looked around him all he could see was a snow-bound wilderness that was gradually darkening. Sporadic flakes were still falling, but there was hardly any wind and Luke felt like a puny speck in a primeval world that was hostile and alien. Rock, snow, ice and wolves. That was what they were up against and it made for the most overwhelming odds. At least they had their mission to find Rock, Luke thought. It must be so much worse for his father and Brett, just lying there waiting.

When he looked up, he saw Finn standing on the summit of the mountain, a lonely figure, holding his goggles in one hand, leaning on his ski sticks, clearly exhausted.

With rising hope, Luke walked the final crest towards the summit, but when he reached Finn, gasping for breath, he found himself gazing down in bitter disappointment at yet another forested valley. Even worse, this time a river cut the valley in half, a river that was a foaming torrent.

Luke gazed down bleakly, unable to judge the distance. There was no sign of the airfield. Had Finn's navigation let them down?

Luke glanced at his cousin and saw him looking perplexed.

"Where's the airfield? Where's Rock?" he mumbled.

"Must be in the next valley." Finn was checking with the air map, fingers clumsy in his ski gloves.

"But that's miles away."

"We'll have to make camp when the light goes. What's the time?"

"Three."

"OK. We'll have to find somewhere sheltered to eat and drink, and then push on down to the valley while we've still got some light."

"You're sure Rock *is* in the next valley?"

"Pretty sure."

"What's that supposed to mean?"

"It means I'm pretty sure," replied Finn irritably, gazing at the air map as if he was looking for something he'd missed.

"But not totally sure?"

Finn ignored him, continuing to study the map. A wave of renewed frustration swept over Luke. Was Finn holding out on him? Did he have knowledge he wouldn't share?

Luke shuddered as he gazed down into the rugged valley and its torrential river. He had never seen such a forbidding sight in his life.

"We need to move fast," said Finn, looking up at the sky. "There's heavy snow coming." He peeled off his ski skins, folded them sticky side together, and put them in his rucksack. Then he clamped his boots rigid again.

Luke gazed at him fearfully as he did the same.

"Let's go," said Finn.

Finn began to ski diagonally across the wide slope that led down to the river. Fortunately the trees had thinned out.

Luke skied in Finn's tracks, finding the going easier at last and slowly his turns became more precise and controlled.

Overconfident now, Luke suddenly turned too sharply, tumbling head over heels and then sliding down with his skis outstretched. Pulling them off, he dragged himself to his feet.

"This is no time for a sleep." Finn had come back for him and his grin was more friendly than sardonic. His mood seemed to have changed yet again.

"Sorry." Luke stumbled to his feet and stood awkwardly, trying to get his skis back on but falling over again, feeling like an idiot.

"Want a hand?" Finn hauled Luke to his feet and helped him back on his skis. "You OK?" he asked.

"I'm fine," said Luke defensively.

"You're doing good."

"Thanks." Luke was amazed at the compliment.

"See those trees?" Finn indicated an isolated cluster of pines. "We'll get some shelter down there and have something to eat."

Luke looked up at the rapidly darkening clouds that seemed to be swirling even lower. "What about the snowstorm?"

"It'll come," said Finn.

"What do we do?"

"Sit it out if we have to. But maybe the storm won't be so bad – we may be able to ski through it. Come on – let's go."

Finn continued to ski down the mountain while Luke proceeded more cautiously, making wider turns and not going so fast.

As they reached the trees, Luke slid to a halt.

"You OK?" asked Finn again and Luke felt comforted. He sounded as if he actually cared.

"I've been thinking about your dad – and mine," said Luke. "They could die of exposure – or the wolves might get them," he added, seeing a mental picture of the pack tearing at the broken branches they had stuffed into the holes in the fuselage.

Finn shook his head. "Wolves don't normally attack without provocation. And I'm sure Rock's in the next valley and we can raise the alarm."

"What are the chances of your being wrong?"

"There aren't any." Finn sounded too glib and Luke wished he would be more realistic with him. He took off his backpack and felt deeply relieved to have lost the dead weight. He rooted for sandwiches and the bottle of water. "Don't drink too much," Finn cautioned him.

"Why not? Can't we melt snow?" asked Luke in surprise.

"We've only got one box of matches and we'll need a fire tonight."

"And tomorrow night?" asked Luke uneasily. "If we take too long, what about your dad and—"

Finn was impatient. "Just trust me, will you? I'm not making it up."

"Sorry." Luke took a bite out of a cheese and tomato sandwich which tasted fantastic. In fact, he had never tasted anything so wonderful in his life.

"We'll have to ration the food too," said Finn.

Luke nodded. His feelings for Finn were mixed. He was far more experienced at survival, but could he read an air map on the ground? Luke bit into the sandwich and chewed at the heavenly stuff inside.

Finn laughed. "I've never seen a guy enjoy a sandwich more than you."

"I'm starving."

"That's why we need to ration."

"I'm sorry—" Luke began.

"What about?"

"You know – your brother and all that."

Finn frowned. "I don't want to talk about it."

"I just wanted to say I was sorry."

"Yeah."

There was a silence, then Luke said, "You say we're not in danger from the wolves?"

"Only if they're hungry."

"What do they live on?"

"Deer and small stuff – like mice and rabbits."

Luke nodded, wanting to be reassured.

"We'd better be moving on. It'll be dark in an hour."

"Can we get across that river?" asked Luke.

"We'll go take a look."

They clicked on their skis again, Luke feeling incredibly stiff and tired.

"How do you feel?" asked Finn.

"I'm OK."

"You shouldn't be. You should feel like I do. Lousy."

Luke gave him a rueful smile. "I didn't want to let you down."

"You haven't."

Luke felt a glow of pleasure. "I'm not as fit as you are."

"You will be," Finn replied.

The threatened snowstorm seemed to have bypassed them and Finn and Luke skied on until the rocky surface of the lower valley brought them to a halt. The thundering of the torrential river was much louder now and they could distinctly hear the dull crunching made by the chunks of ice and the broken branches which were being swept along with the current.

There seemed no possible way across.

"We'll have to work our way downstream," Finn shouted above the roar of the water.

Luke could hardly hear him, but got the message as Finn took off his skis and began strapping them to his pack. Luke did the same, snapping the catch on his boots as he did so. Then they began to tread carefully over the treacherous mix of snow and ice and rock that ran alongside the fast flowing river.

Several times Luke slipped, only just managing to steady himself.

"Be careful!" shouted Finn, glancing back at him

and then almost slipping himself.

Picking his way along, Luke felt the sense of proper companionship – of friends challenging the odds, of being together with a common cause, trusting and depending on each other. The feeling was exhilarating, but Luke wondered if the companionship was just in his mind. Maybe this was his fantasy, like Finn's about his brother.

They were now heading towards a bend where the river narrowed, causing the torrent to surge forward ferociously into a rocky gorge.

As they began to round the bend, Finn, still in front, cried out in surprise.

"What is it?"

"See for yourself!"

Spray was rising from the river now as the flow lashed the rocks, forming a mist through which Luke could only very dimly detect a familiar shape. What was it? Luke screwed up his eyes and tried to make out what was so familiar and yet so impossible to identify.

"It's a bridge!" he yelled suddenly. "I don't believe it. Someone's built a bridge."

Sure enough he was right. It was incredible.

Finn was also staring ahead in amazement. Then Finn turned and grabbed Luke's shoulder, spinning him round. Grinning at each other in delight, they slapped hands.

Surely the bridge completely vindicated Finn's navigation, thought Luke in wild and hopeful excitement. It would be too small to be marked on the air map. But surely with a bridge, civilisation couldn't be that far away. Finn had been right after all and Rock *must* be in the next valley.

Luke shouted congratulations, yelling praise until he was hoarse. Finn was looking intensely relieved.

"You were right!" Luke yelled above the roaring of the torrent.

"What?"

"You were right. Rock *must* be in the next valley."

They both began to move ahead, taking care not to lose their balance and plunge into the raging river where ice blocks were colliding with a series of dull thumps.

When he got closer to the bridge, however, Finn paused and swore, and when Luke joined him he felt a pang of disappointment. Made of wood, the middle of the bridge had partly broken away, leaving just a narrow section of cracked timber. It would be like walking a tightrope, thought Luke – a tightrope that stretched for at least three or four metres.

"Any good at doing a balancing act?" asked Finn. He was all too clearly depressed and agitated. Then he pulled himself together. "We're going to have to cross somehow. The good news is the bridge must have been built for tourists – which means we're nearer to Rock than we thought." Finn sounded as if he was trying to reassure himself and a doubt crept into Luke's mind yet again. But he tried to block it out. "We'll go for it," said Finn.

"Let's do that," said Luke, trying to conceal his anxiety.

Snow

As Luke looked up at the bridge, another anxiety surfaced. Surely this couldn't be a bridge for tourists? Civilisation couldn't be that near – not with a wolf pack on the loose. Then he cheered up a little. Maybe it was used by the ranger and his team.

"Ready?" asked Finn rather shakily and Luke saw how afraid he was. That's a first, Luke thought, but the fact that Finn was openly showing his fear for once, actually undermined Luke's confidence even further.

"Don't you think we should try going further

downstream?" suggested Luke.

"I can't hear you," Finn bellowed impatiently.

Luke was just about to repeat his plea when he realised that the sky had clouded over again and large snowflakes were settling on his goggles. Luke tore them off and let them hang round his neck. "OK," he shouted. "Who's going first?"

Then, to Luke's horror, Finn said, "Do you want to give it a try? I don't have much of a head for heights – not that kind of height anyway – and I'd feel better if you'd suss it out first."

Luke felt sick with apprehension and stood rooted to the slippery bank. Finn was relying on him to take the lead. Maybe this was a test, or maybe he was genuinely afraid. Either way, Luke had to go first and this was the very last thing he wanted to do.

"OK?" asked Finn brusquely, belatedly attempting to cover up his own insecurities. "I'll stay close behind you."

The snow was falling heavily now and the bridge was disappearing in what was fast becoming a white-out.

"Shouldn't we wait until this snowstorm's over?"

Luke suggested.

"We can't – it's going to get dark soon, and there's no cover here. It's all ice. There's nowhere we can dig in – and the other side's much more sheltered."

Luke could just pick out a tree-line beyond the bridge. Finn was right.

He began to move towards the rickety bridge, the snow making his eyes sting. Dimly, Luke could make out a wooden handrail on each side and soon there were planks beneath his feet. He tested them and they seemed firm enough.

"OK?" asked Finn who was just behind him.

"Er – they seem all right." Despite having resented Finn's bossiness, Luke was unprepared for changing roles with him. Leadership was a new experience for Luke.

Below them, the river thundered into the gorge, but Luke cautiously moved on. The planks beneath his feet began to feel increasingly unsafe, and he saw he was now approaching the point where only one single plank spanned the torrent. Worse still, the handrail had fallen away on both sides and there was nothing – absolutely nothing – to hang on to.

Luke hesitated, mouth dry and heart hammering.

The snow swirled down faster.

Why couldn't Finn have gone first?

Luke paused. He had become so used to relying on Finn that the very idea that he should act on his own initiative was totally alien to him.

"I'm sorry," said Finn from behind him, as if reading his thoughts.

"What for?"

"I've just got no head for some kinds of heights – I don't mind mountains, or even a mountain slope, but this is different."

It certainly was, thought Luke. Below them in the gorge the river was boiling amongst the rocks, and spray was shooting upwards to meet the thick falling snow.

Luke stared ahead at the rotten plank and then back down at the misty vapour and driving snow. If he slipped and plunged into that icy water, Luke knew he wouldn't have the slightest chance of survival.

Then the blanket of snow seemed to lessen a little, and as he glanced over his shoulder Luke saw them.

"What's the matter?" asked Finn anxiously. "What is it?"

"They're back."

"Who?"

"The wolves."

They both craned their necks round to see behind them, holding on to the last piece of handrail.

"You're right," said Finn.

There seemed to be four of them, but the conditions were so poor it wasn't really possible to count. All they could make out were dark shapes padding along the riverbank.

The wolves stopped perhaps fifty metres away from them, crowding together, their lithe bodies still as they gazed down at the freezing water. Then the snow thickened again and the pack was lost to sight.

"They're following us," said Luke.

Finn said nothing, as if not trusting himself to speak.

"Maybe they're hungry," added Luke ominously.

"Maybe they just want to find a place to drink." Finn's words sounded forced, and Luke wondered what Finn had really wanted to say.

Suddenly Luke had a more comforting thought. "They won't be able to get across the river, will they? Or do you think they'll use the bridge?" The thought of balancing on the narrow plank with a wolf close behind made him sick with fear.

"Do you want me to go in front?" asked Finn. "We don't have much time. The snow's getting worse and the light's going."

He was right. Soon they wouldn't be able to see what they were doing. Yet Luke still hesitated. It would be great to hand over to Finn, but he knew he couldn't. He *had* to take the lead. It was his turn.

"Luke – for—"

"I'm going." He began to edge forward cautiously and then ran out of handrail.

The snow swirled, his eyes smarted, and Luke was shivering. He came to a grinding halt. Then he began to move slowly and hesitantly backwards.

"You're going the wrong way," said Finn drily.

"There's nothing to hold on to."

"That's too bad."

"What am I going to do?" Why didn't they have a plan, thought Luke indignantly. How am I meant to cross?

"Sit down!" bellowed Finn above the torrent.

"What?"

"Sit down! Go over on your butt." Finn was both commanding and impatient.

Luke didn't move.

"Go on."

Carefully balancing the weight of his backpack and skis, Luke sat down and began to edge towards the last remaining plank, straddling the rotten wood with his legs, testing his weight.

"OK?" asked Finn anxiously.

Luke gazed down into the gorge. The roar sounded like the voice of some primeval monster.

"Sort of."

"Move!"

The plank didn't actually feel rotten, at least not yet anyway. Luke pushed himself forwards, his legs gripping the rough sides of the wood, all too conscious of the weight of his rucksack and skis. He could see nothing ahead of him except a wall of snowflakes. He couldn't estimate how far he would have to go before he found the handrail again – and would be able to pull himself to safety.

As he inched his way along, the plank seemed

increasingly spongy. He was still wearing his ski gloves and wished he wasn't – they didn't give him enough grip.

"What are you doing?" Finn's voice suddenly rapped from behind.

Luke cautiously turned his head but there was no sign of his cousin at all in the swirling snowflakes.

"What *are* you doing?" Finn repeated, his voice threatening.

"I'm walking the plank," snapped Luke. "What do you *think* I'm doing?"

"Well, get on with it then."

"Huh!" This wasn't the time for an argument – Luke's backpack was a dead weight now with snow piling up on top, making his load even heavier. Still he inched along, but where was the opposite handrail?

The sensation of sponginess increased and Luke froze as the plank vibrated and he heard a cracking sound. He stared ahead, only seeing snow.

"What was that?"

"How should I know?"

"I'd better start..." began Finn.

"No! The plank won't take both our weights."

For the first time Luke was in command. "Stay there."

Cautiously, Luke began to inch his way along the plank again. His every move across what was left of the bridge was becoming increasingly painful, and the weight of his backpack and skis made him unbalanced. Several times, Luke had to stop and grip hard with his knees to prevent himself turning over.

Then, just as he was beginning to despair, Luke saw the insubstantial, snow-covered handrail and then gradually the rest of the undamaged bridge came into view.

Luke struggled on, moving even more cautiously as his exhaustion caught up with him. At last, with a sigh of relief, he was able to grab the handrail. It immediately gave way with a sickening splitting sound.

Luke almost turned over on the rotten plank, still holding a broken piece of the rail in his hand. Desperately gripping even tighter with his knees, he managed to straighten up, and throwing away the broken handrail, grabbed the snow-laden plank in front of him. He was gasping for breath and, as the shock hit him, his stomach contracted and a little moan of fear escaped from his lips.

"What's happening?" yelled Finn.

Luke couldn't reply.

"Are you all right?"

"Yes."

"What are you doing?"

"Sitting about. Trying to keep the right way up." Luke was so traumatised that he had to continue joking; it was the only way he was going to get through this.

Luke moved forward again until he was at the end of the plank. Then, slowly, carefully, he reached out and managed to grab a lower section of the handrail that held firm. He tested it time and again until he was sure he could drag himself off the plank on to what remained of the bridge.

"Are – you – OK?" Finn's anxiety was increasing.

"Yes." Luke grabbed the firm section of wood and gave an almighty pull. Clumsily, still feeling he might roll upside-down at any moment, he managed to pull himself to safety and on to the ground on the other side of the bridge. He staggered to his feet and took off his backpack and skis. He then struggled back up on to the bridge, hooking his ankles round a lower section of the handrail and yelling, "Finn, I'm waiting to grab you! You'll have to sit on the plank and pull yourself along. Can you do that?"

"Of course I can."

"Be careful. For God's sake, be careful. The plank's rotten."

"I'm on my way."

Luke could see nothing in the heavy snow that was now settling on him like a shroud. He leant as far forward as he dared, holding out his hands until he realised that he'd never get an effective grip on Finn with ski gloves on. Hurriedly, aware that he had very little time, Luke sat upright, tearing off his gloves and shoving them in his pocket. He then leant over again, his hands already beginning to go numb with cold.

Panic swept over him. Was he getting frostbite? Maybe he should put his ski gloves on again. Luke dithered, and then decided against the idea. Then he changed his mind and was about to pull the gloves out of his pocket when he saw a blurred shape in the white-out ahead of him. Finn was within a couple of feet of him, looking as top-heavy as Luke had. Then there came another cracking sound and to his horror

Luke saw that the plank Finn was on was slowly splitting in two.

"Throw yourself forwards!" he yelled.

"What?" Clearly Finn had no idea what was happening.

"Throw yourself forwards. Now!"

Finn did as Luke told him, and Luke just managed to grab his wrists, gripping them tightly, bracing himself to take Finn's weight.

"You're OK," Luke gasped.

"The plank's breaking up." Finn gazed at him through the snowfall and Luke could see the desperation in his eyes.

"I'm pulling you in."

At that very moment the plank gave way.

Luke kept his grip on his cousin's wrists, his arms almost being dragged out of their sockets. If his ankles hadn't been gripped around the bottom of the handrail, he would have plunged down into the gorge with Finn.

The weight of Finn's body, skisuit, backpack and skis were almost too much to bear, but somehow Luke still clung on while Finn, with a survivor's instinct, flipped up his legs again and again until he managed to wrap them around what remained of the single plank. Luke's hands were still locked round Finn's wrists, but they were now in a deadlock and could make no progress at all.

Finn's face was bathed in sweat as he desperately tried to inch his way forward, but his backpack was weighing him down too heavily. Luke realised that only their combined determination was keeping Finn out of the gorge, but his muscles were so painful that he felt as if red-hot needles were shooting up and down his arms.

"This isn't going to work," gasped Finn.

"Of course it is," yelled Luke, the pain intensifying. The river seemed to roar even louder from its deadly gorge.

"Let me go."

"Shut up." The bottom of the handrail gave an ominous creak. "Try – and – pull – yourself – along."

With the veins standing out in his forehead, Finn made an attempt to move, but only managed to unlock his legs from around the rotten plank.

"No!" he hissed.

"Yes!" yelled Luke. "You've got to try. So try now."

With an immense final effort, Finn dragged his legs along the plank and then came to another halt. "Let me go."

"No."

"Do what I say. I can grab the struts under the bridge and pull myself along."

"It's too dodgy!" yelled Luke.

"Do what I say."

But Luke only let go of one wrist while Finn shot out the other arm and grabbed the underside wooden strut of the bridge. Miraculously it held.

"Now let go my other wrist."

Luke did as he was told, and with his free hand Finn just managed to grab the strut and swing down underneath the bridge, his gear a dead weight, dragging him down. Then, hand over hand, ankle over ankle, he hauled himself from one strut to another, pulling hard, the veins standing out even more in his forehead, the sweat pouring down his face.

Luke backed off the bridge to ease the weight, and Finn continued to clamber along until he reached the opposite bank where there was a gradual incline and a few footholds. He then let go of the struts. With a cry of anguish he lay on the rising frozen ground, gasping for air. Below him, the river monster seemed to howl in disappointment.

Luke scrambled down to Finn, and together they sat at the river's edge, gazing down at the thundering gorge in silence.

Exultation took over. Finn gave a great war cry of relief and Luke did the same as the snowflakes continued to settle on their heads.

"You saved my life," said Finn.

"You saved your own life."

"I couldn't have done it without you."

"You'd have done the same for me." Luke now knew this was true, and there was a feeling of bonding with his cousin at last.

"This is warrior training," said Finn.

"What do you mean?"

"The young men of Indian tribes – they used to be sent out into the wilderness when they were about our age."

"What for?"

"To prove themselves, to stop being kids and grow

up. To be men."

"Do you reckon we've passed the test?"

"We haven't got there yet," said Finn cryptically.

Luke realised that Finn was right. He glanced at his watch. It was just after four and the light was fading fast. "What happens now?" he asked.

"I guess we should walk until dark – which won't be long."

"Is there a chance of a sighting of Rock?"

"We'll have to climb for a long while." Finn sounded doubtful. Then he looked up at the sky. "I reckon the snow's lessening. Maybe it'll stop. That would give us a little more time."

They both got slowly to their feet.

"I can hardly stand," said Luke. His legs felt so weak they were trembling.

"Me too," replied Finn. "You know. All this – I'll never feel the same again."

Luke nodded. He understood.

Visions

Slowly the snow began to lessen
and the twilight deepened.

As they plodded uphill Luke began to feel increasingly optimistic. If they could only get to the top of the mountain they might be able to see the airfield. He imagined the runway lights glimmering in the darkness, light aircraft parked near the hangars, cars drawn up in a car park, the control tower and a cafe with a Coca-Cola sign.

The vision began to obsess him, becoming more detailed as he added a hotel and a helipad where a fully equipped rescue helicopter was waiting to fly to the wreck of the Cessna and rescue Dad and Brett. Everything would soon be straightened out, made miraculously all right.

Because he was so distracted, Luke tripped several times and almost plunged into the snow drifts that had built up on the gently sloping side of the mountain.

"You OK?" asked Finn.

Luke nodded and went on to describe his vision, but Finn didn't seem very impressed. "I wouldn't build up your hopes," he muttered, but Luke was already imagining them skiing down a gentle slope towards the welcoming lights of civilisation and in particular the Coca-Cola sign over the cafe. Never in his life had he craved a drink and maybe half a dozen doughnuts so much.

Anger and frustration suddenly flared up in Luke and he turned on Finn accusingly. "You got the map-reading wrong," he yelled.

Finn was immediately on the defensive. "It's difficult to tell. The air map isn't detailed enough. But I know we're on the right compass bearing."

Well, it certainly wasn't this valley – and maybe it

wouldn't even be the next. How many more hours, days, would they have to walk? Meanwhile, their fathers were trapped in the wrecked plane. Finn said wolves didn't usually attack humans. But their fathers were injured and helpless. Would the wolves break in through the barricades in the fuselage? Or would Sam and Brett simply freeze to death?

Luke remembered a project at school about Captain Scott and his ill-fated expedition to the South Pole and how the whole team were found dead in their tents. Before the tragedy, Captain Oates had walked out into the Antarctic wastes to die alone, sacrificing himself so there would be more food for the other members of the expedition. *"I'm just going for a short walk,"* said Oates over and over in Luke's mind. *"I'm just going for a short walk."* He turned angrily on Finn again. "So, is Rock going to be in the next valley – or not?"

"I'm not sure." Finn didn't sound defensive now, only matter-of-fact. "All I *do* know for sure is that we're on the right compass bearing. We have to be."

Luke's disappointment was painful, but his fear was even greater. What if their fathers couldn't make it? What if reaching Rock just took too long?

"Let's set up for the night in the forest," said Finn, glancing up at the sky. "At least the snow isn't coming down so fast now."

"And tomorrow?"

"We keep to the compass bearing." Finn seemed curiously detached, as if his feelings were on hold.

"Can't we push on at night?" asked Luke. "We've got a torch and we can keep to your compass bearing."

'We need rest.'

'What about my dad? And yours?'

Finn shrugged. 'We're no good to them if we're exhausted. We need rest to tackle this sort of terrain. We'll get some sleep, and start again at dawn."

They made straight for the trees ahead of them, and half an hour later arrived in the shadow of the forest. Most of the trees had a great deal of snow in their upper branches, but there wasn't much on the ground. Then Luke heard a steady dripping sound and realised the temperature was rising, if only by a few degrees.

"We're going to be lying in pools of water all night," he complained.

"Not if we make a bivouac, thatch the outside and

put the tent up inside."

"*Thatch*?" asked Luke. "What do you mean?"

"What we need to do is find a really big, wide tree. Then get some strong fallen branches and stack them round the tree as densely as we can to make the bivouac as waterproof as possible. Then we put the tent up inside."

As they took off their gear, a wild rage suddenly filled Luke, and he wanted to lash out at Finn, to punish him for being so detached, for not saying anything about their fathers' plight. They could be dead even now, but Finn didn't seem to care. Luke kicked the trunk of a tree with his heavy ski boot, imagining he was kicking Finn.

"What are you doing that for?" Finn sounded as if he was admonishing a naughty child, and Luke's anger flared out of control.

"You don't care."

"About what?"

"Our fathers."

"Don't be stupid."

"I'm not stupid." Luke could hear a shrillness in his voice that he didn't like, and felt a flicker of shame which was soon swamped by the sheer force of his anger. "And I don't trust you."

"Don't trust me?"

"Can you *really* read a compass?"

"Of course I can." Finn was still admonishing, still detached. Ignoring Luke's rage, he began picking up a series of dead branches and testing them over his knee to make sure they weren't too rotten. "I can definitely read a compass," said Finn patiently. "I've been able to read a compass since I was five years old."

"Yeah?" Luke spat out.

"Yeah."

Finn turned his back on him and Luke kicked the tree again. Then he hurled himself at Finn, rugby-tackling him to the ground. They began to roll about the glade until Finn got on top and pinned Luke's shoulders down with his knees.

"Feel better now, do you?" he gasped.

Luke said nothing, trying to turn his head away to avoid Finn's triumphant gaze, but was unable to do so.

Seeing that Luke wasn't going to rebel any longer Finn got off him, and returned to his hunt for strong branches.

Luke lay on the ground for a while, his rage spent. Then, without any further comment, he joined Finn in his hunt for wood.

They worked for over half an hour, building up wood stocks for the night, determined to make a fire big enough to deter wild animals. Eventually, Finn reckoned they'd collected enough.

With considerable expertise, Finn built up a wigwam of twigs, packed larger pieces of wood around them and applied one, single match. Soon the fire was blazing and they both sat round the flames, exhausted and silent.

Later, they lay in their sleeping bags in the same total silence. Luke felt devastated at his attack on Finn. He'd never been violent before. So why now? OK, they were in a bad situation, but it didn't call for that. He'd cracked up.

"I'm sorry," he eventually blurted out.

"Forget it. You still saved my life." But Finn's voice was distant and detached again, as if saving a life didn't really matter, as if it didn't mean anything.

Then Luke heard the sound of wolves howling. Finn sat up. The sound abruptly broke off, and then began again. This time it seemed much nearer.

"Suppose they're hungry?" ventured Luke.

"Why should they be?" Finn was dismissive, but there was now a note of what Luke considered unnatural excitement in his voice. Or was he just imagining it?

"Let's take a look."

"What?"

"Why not?" As Finn pulled himself out of his sleeping bag and opened the flap of the tent, bright moonlight streamed into the bivouac. We're not giving ourselves a chance! thought Luke.

Then he gasped when he saw a half circle of crouching wolves with their ears laid back. There must have been about a dozen of them, bathed in moonlight, their fur ash-grey, eyes glinting. Their wrinkled lips were parted, showing their sharp fangs. A few of the wolves were ominously sniffing the air, ears pricked. They were some way from the fire, as if they respected the flames, knowing that they were powerful and could hurt.

"I don't think they're interested in us," whispered Finn.

As if to bear out his words, the wolves began to play with a stick, tossing it high in the air, taking turns to catch it, leaping and jumping as high as they could, as if soaring up to the crescent moon that was now riding high in the sky with the jewel-like stars.

Finn seemed to be taking only an academic interest, and Luke noticed he was watching with a kind of respectful admiration as the wolves continued to play.

"Karl used to say his prayers," muttered Finn. "So he stands a chance, doesn't he?"

"I don't understand," replied Luke, who was now deeply afraid.

Then, Luke saw a young wolf pad into the glade, and start to join in the game, rolling over on the ground with little yelping sounds when he failed to catch the stick which was being tossed into the air.

Eventually, the young wolf gave up the game and began to sniff round the glade, gradually loping nearer and nearer to the bivouac.

"How old is he?" whispered Luke, trying to join in Finn's mood of calm contemplation, rather than give way to the terror he was feeling inside.

"Hard to say." Finn paused, keeping his eyes fixed on the young wolf which was still steadily moving towards the bivouac.

Finn seemed to be somewhere else – in another place a long way from Luke.

The young wolf padded closer to them and made a kind of muted howling sound. Then the rest of the pack pricked up their ears.

Teeth

The pack were now gathered around the bivouac and one of the adults made a low growling noise as they stood in their semicircle. Luke could smell a rankness in the air that was close and claustrophobic. The smell of wolf.

"That's the alpha male," whispered Finn. "He's the leader. What he does, the pack follows."

Sure enough, other members of the pack began to growl, baring their strong white teeth, saliva running down their shaggy jaws as they continued to edge nearer in formation, their tails held high in the air, their fur bushed out so that they looked twice their normal size.

"What are we going to do?" Luke whispered. "How can we keep them away?"

Finn gave him a cursory glance and then looked away.

"For God's sake, Finn—"

"What is it?"

"They're going to attack us. They're coming in for the kill." Luke's voice ended on a half sob.

"I'm not sure—" Finn paused.

"What are we—" began Luke.

"Sit still."

"Is that all?"

"That's all we *can* do." But Finn didn't seem frightened. It was almost as if he was as curious as the wolves. But was it just curiosity, wondered Luke, or was he really disturbed?

The wolves stiffened and turned, sensing a presence. Suddenly, stupidly, a fox ran across the snow at high speed – but not fast enough to escape the pack which circled him, until the fox was running in ever-decreasing circles as the wolves closed in.

For a moment nothing happened. The fox crouched down in the middle of the circle, eyes searching for a means of escape, but finding none. Then the pack silently fell on their quarry, some of them giving little yelping sounds.

Luke turned away as he heard the crunching of bone. Then he looked back, as if compelled to watch the pack ripping at the fox. For a while the wolves fed and then they backed away, leaving the remains bathed in wan moonlight.

Luke gasped. All that was left of the fox was a bloodied pile of fur.

"Karl," muttered Luke.

"What about him?" said Finn.

There seemed no answer, no comfort Luke could give Finn. Anything he said would be pathetic. Luke just gave a grim nod, wondering whether the terrible scene they had just witnessed had jerked Finn back to reality.

"Should we move on?" Luke asked.

"We must wait till dawn."

"Do the wolves sleep in the day?"

Finn shook his head. "Not necessarily. They could come back any time." He began to talk very fast. "They could come back for us. Try and carry us off to live with them, like they did with Karl."

Luke's heart sank. Now Finn was afraid of the wolves too. But he still didn't seem to understand what must have happened to Karl.

But Finn had turned his back on Luke and was heading for his sleeping bag. "We'd better try and get some sleep," he said in a sudden return to normality.

Then they both heard a distant howling, followed by barking.

"We're safe," said Finn, turning over in his sleeping bag. "They've made another kill."

Safe? But for how long, wondered Luke as he watched the crackling flames of the fire – the fire that had completely failed to deter the wolves.

After a few hours of broken and restless sleep, Luke woke to a grey dawn and a pounding headache. For a while he couldn't work out where he was, and gazed in bewilderment out of the tent flap at the broken branches that made up the bivouac. It was the only barrier between them and the outside world.

He shivered, as the memories of yesterday came rushing back into his mind. Images of wolves, broken bridges and wrecked aircraft filled him with intense pain and confusion. Slowly the traumatic experiences began to sort themselves out into some kind of chronology and he turned to see Finn lying beside him, snoring slightly, his face composed, as if he was at home in bed.

Luke felt sure that he was going to wake up to an equally unpleasant shock and decided to try and make it easier for him. Gently, he shook Finn awake.

"What—"

"We're heading for Rock," said Luke hurriedly. "And we're going to make it."

Finn yawned and crawled out of the bivouac, closely followed by Luke. In the cold grey light of dawn, they were confronted by the pile of bloodied fur.

"What now?" asked Luke, and Finn began to bluster.

"I don't understand it. The compass bearing has to be right. We can't be lost. Not with Dad—" He suddenly stopped speaking, realising he had already said too much.

But Luke's fears were aroused and he forgot to be comforting. "*Could* there have been a mistake?"

"No." Finn had snapped back to being his old closed-off self. "We took a compass bearing so we have to be heading in the right direction."

"*You* took a compass bearing," Luke corrected him.

"Something I've been doing for years – and I've never made a mistake." Finn was defensive.

"Always a first time," said Luke gloomily.

"No way." Finn turned back to the bivouac. "Come on. Let's have some food and hit the trail."

The last of the sandwiches were stale and hard now, but they both ate them ravenously, checking out how much food and drink they had left. The result was: two apples, four hot cans, one orange and about half a bottle of water each.

That doesn't seem very much, thought Luke, unless, of course, we make Rock today. But he could see that the weather conditions were still poor, which wouldn't help. Were they really way off course for Rock, or even just going round in circles?

Finn seemed edgy and Luke kept nursing the

thought that he *had* made some kind of navigational mistake and wasn't letting on. Suddenly to know the truth seemed absolutely essential.

"It doesn't matter," Luke began as Finn checked over the equipment.

"What doesn't?"

"If you made a mistake."

"I didn't."

"You could tell me now."

"Why don't you just shut up?"

"I'm only trying to help."

"By doubting every word I say?"

"It's easy to make a mistake."

"I didn't. Rock's just further than I thought. It's difficult to tell from an air map. What might seem a short hop in a plane is a mighty long walk on the ground."

"What are the chances of getting there today?"

"Good." But somehow Finn still sounded unsure.

"We're low on rations."

"Don't state the obvious."

"I'd just like to know, that's all."

"So would I," said Finn dismissively. "Now let's get

going and the less we talk the better."

"What about the wolves?"

"What about them?"

"Do you think they're going to follow us?"

"You're really paranoid, aren't you?"

Luke shrugged. There didn't seem any more to say, and Finn seemed to be back to normal. But the wolves' appearance last night seemed like a threat – the promise of something terrible.

Luke could feel the tension increasing between him and Finn as they dragged themselves uphill, making slow progress, stiff from a night of discomfort. The long slope up the mountain seemed endless. He knows I don't trust him, thought Luke. He could have made a mistake, but even if he has, he's not going to admit it, is he? The unsettling anxieties undermined Luke's concentration and gradually he fell behind until he lost sight of Finn amongst the trees. *You're paranoid*, came Finn's voice in his mind. *You're paranoid*.

"Finn!" Luke yelled out, but there was no reply.

Swearing, he tried to push himself faster, but a huge wave of fatigue swept over him.

"Finn!"

But there was still no answer and Luke began to panic. If he lost Finn – that would be it. The trees were particularly dense halfway up the mountain and although it was now almost nine o'clock the morning was overcast, without the slightest hint of sun.

Then he heard a rustling sound.

Luke came to a halt, peering into the gloom.

The rustling sound came again and then stopped, as if something was moving towards him and then waiting.

Was he being followed?

"Finn!" Luke didn't dare to raise his voice above a whisper, yet he knew there was no chance of being heard. "Finn!"

He listened, convinced that something was listening to him. Or was it all in his imagination? Then he heard the rustling again and this time a grey wolf broke cover.

Their eyes met, the wolf's eyes a strange yellow.

Then the wolf turned back into the trees and was lost to sight, the rustling sound fading away to nothing.

Luke stood staring, listening to the silence.

He'd lost Finn, was being followed by the pack and

had no will to continue.

Then there was a sudden flurry of snow. "What are you staring at?" asked Finn furiously, coming to a halt.

"I saw a wolf."

"Good for you. They live here. Remember?"

"It was tracking me."

Luke could see the contempt in Finn's gaze.

"We could be eaten alive."

"You won't. You're too much skin and bone. I'm the one they'd like on the menu. If they're hungry, that is."

There was a long silence between them as Luke imagined the wolves as a lurking presence, ready to pounce.

Suddenly Finn seemed to soften. "I was really worried."

"What about?"

"You."

"I'm sorry. I lagged behind. I won't do it again."

"You might if you're as tired as I am."

Luke wished he could have been as honest as Finn had just been with him. But then Finn continued impatiently, "Somehow we've got to keep going."

The howling started without warning and was near.

Where were they? wondered Luke. Then the howling stopped as suddenly as it had begun.

"You were right," said Finn. "The pack's around. But don't let that get to you."

"They'll only attack us if they're hungry," Luke mimicked.

Finn shrugged. "They had a kill last night."

"So maybe they got their appetites back."

Finn looked away and Luke wondered to what extent Finn had been masking his fear. But, somehow, Finn's small show of anxiety made Luke feel stronger and more resolute.

"OK," he said. "Let's get going." Luke surprised himself. That was the phrase Finn normally used.

The howling came again. This time the sound was on a number of different notes and much nearer.

They're playing with us, thought Luke. We're just a game to them.

Avalanche

They were walking sideways up a steep slope when Luke first heard the low rumbling.

"What's that?" he demanded, but Finn didn't reply, gazing up intently.

"That's all we need," he muttered, trying to twist himself round, backing away to the trees.

"What do you mean?"

"Move!" yelled Finn. "Get into the tree cover. Now!"

Clumsily, Luke tried to turn, but lost his balance and fell over at an awkward angle.

"Move!" Finn yelled again, but as Luke struggled to get up the rumbling sound became louder. Finn raced back to Luke's side, attempting to haul him to his feet. But as he was looking past Luke, he gave a wild cry of fear. Luke saw what was happening. A vast wall of snow was heading straight for them.

"It's an avalanche," yelled Luke.

"You've got there at last," shouted Finn above the rumbling. And then the snow was on top of them, in their eyes and ears as it carried them back downhill, scarcely able to breathe, suffocated by the stuff, the rumbling now a roar.

Suddenly everything went white and Luke couldn't see anything. He felt himself roll over and over while the snow deepened about him and he fought for air. Frantically he tried to beat the stuff off, but it was so heavy and there was such a lot of it that he made little impression.

Terrified, virtually unable to breathe, he still fought back as hard as he could. Suddenly and surprisingly, he found he was making progress, the weight on top of him lightening until, heart pounding, his head broke through the crust of snow and he was able to gaze about him.

Where was Finn? There was no sign of him on the slope. Had he made the trees? But how could he have done? Neither of them had had any time.

Then Luke saw an arm poking up through the snow.

"Finn!" he shouted. Had the arm moved a fraction? Was there a signal? Then it sank from sight.

The panic spread inside him, and struggling to his feet Luke raced towards the place where he thought the hand had vanished. He began to dig, tearing off his gloves because they seemed too clumsy, the searing cold making his fingers numb. To his joy Luke saw Finn's raised arm again, scrabbling at the heavy snow. Shouting out Finn's name Luke continued to dig, gasping, yelling and imploring Finn to stay alive.

Eventually he began to uncover a shoulder and then Finn's head. His features seemed frozen, eyes staring ahead as if he was already dead, but slowly his blue lips began to move and, unbelievably, he said, "What kept you?"

"You're alive! How did you keep breathing?"

"With difficulty. There must have been some lighter snow in the fall. Anyway, I managed to breathe. Just."

Luke worked on until Finn was able to clamber out

of the snow and look up the hill, his teeth chattering, body shaking.

"There could be more unstable snow up there. We'd better get back into the tree-line and approach the summit from that side. At least the trees will break up any more falls."

Checking their skins they began to edge across to the trees, walking at an angle, slowly descending.

"Thanks," said Finn at last when they reached the trees. "That's the second time you've saved my life."

As they cautiously began to ski, Luke was sure he saw stealthy movement in the pines below, but despite his fears about a prowling pack, Luke found he was skiing more confidently. This time the boys stayed close together, weaving their way through the trees, sometimes almost clipping them, but always managing to take avoiding action at the last moment.

Despite their predicament, Luke felt a thrill of elation as the trees flashed past. Icicles hung from the branches, and as they brushed them they cracked into dozens of blue shards, hitting the ground and forming a trail.

Luke's hopes rose at their rapid progress. In what

seemed no time at all they reached the other side of the slope to the summit, which was full of soft, deep snow which came up to their knees.

Here, in much worse conditions for skiing, another battle began as they slowly pushed their way through the drifts, crampons on their boots, skis strapped to their backpacks, startling small animals which rushed for cover. There were prints everywhere, but Luke was reassured by the fact they were too small to be those of the wolves.

It was only when they were able to put on their skis and skins again and began to trudge slowly up the hill, where the trees were greater in number and the snow less deep, that Luke heard, or thought he heard, more rustling from amongst the pines.

He decided, however, to keep his fears to himself. Glancing at his watch, Luke saw the time was just after twelve. Finn was waiting for him and they stopped to have a hot can of stew. Finn pierced the three holes in the top with the nail provided, and then they had to wait for five minutes, mouths watering, before pulling the ring that lifted the lid. The stew tasted wonderful. Luke savoured each mouthful as if he was eating something exotic and utterly sustaining.

Soon they were pressing on again, and although he would have found the long climb up the rocky slopes extremely arduous yesterday, today Luke almost overtook Finn as they forged on upwards through the pines, determined they would get to the top before sunset. Then Rock would surely be revealed to them in the broad sweep of the next valley. It was only a matter of time.

Once again Luke's vision took over, centred on the airfield cafe with the Coca-Cola sign. It played out like a movie in Luke's mind. He and Finn went inside to sit at a table where a waitress brought them mugs of hot chocolate which they drained to the last drop. Then she served them steak and hash browns, followed by pancakes and maple syrup.

Directly the fantasy meal was finished, the waitress reappeared and served it all over again. As Luke mentally relished each different flavour, he suddenly saw how a fantasy could appear completely real and become an obsession. Absorbed in his own thoughts, Luke no longer registered the rustling sound until it became a padding which couldn't be ignored. Staring round anxiously, he came to a sudden halt.

The young wolf was a few metres in front of him, staring up at him intently, and for a moment Luke had the unnerving feeling it was trying to convey something.

Finn also came to a halt and whispered, "Don't move."

Luke stayed where he was, trembling now, staring into the blue eyes of the wolf, wondering when the rest of the pack would emerge from the dark pines.

Then with a broken branch in his hand, Finn headed towards the young wolf, yelling fiercely at the top of his voice.

For a moment the wolf snarled and held its ground, but as Finn advanced the creature lost its nerve and began to pad and then to lope away towards the tree cover.

Luke began to sweat.

"You OK?" asked Finn.

"No."

"He was just curious."

"And hungry," said Luke. "The rest of the pack must be in those trees somewhere, picking their moment to come in for the kill."

"Remember, wolves don't work like that."

"How do you know that for sure?"

Finn shrugged. "I've had some experience of them, don't forget."

For a minute Luke stared at him in silence, but he was now too afraid to be cautious, too desperate not to mention Karl.

"They dragged your brother out of a tent. They must have been hungry then."

"Not necessarily," said Finn. Then he paused, as if working out some kind of rationale. "They couldn't have been that hungry – not hungry enough to kill Karl."

Luke could see drops of sweat standing out on Finn's forehead. "Then why did they drag him out?"

"We don't know that they did."

"There was blood—"

"So?" Finn was beginning to shake. "*So?*"

"We'd better move on," said Luke, taking the lead again.

"OK." Finn was staring at him in some distress, and showing no signs of movement at all. Luke wondered what he should do.

"Will we see the airfield in the next valley?"

Finn was silent.

"Do you think we'll see the airfield in the next valley?" Luke asked again, but Finn ignored him.

There was a long silence.

Then Luke repeated uneasily, "We'd better push on."

Finn started to climb the gradually ascending slope and Luke followed, now finding more difficulty in keeping up with him. All his new-found energy seemed to have been sapped. He couldn't even summon up his own fantasy of the cafe with the Coca-Cola sign.

"Don't leave me behind again," Luke shouted.

Again, Finn didn't reply.

Summit

Although it had stopped snowing now, the sky remained overcast and a bitter wind was blowing down the mountainside and straight into their faces, freezing over their goggles and leaving icicles on the hoods of their skisuits.

Luke vaguely remembered the phrase 'wind-chill factor', but it had made little impact when heard on a TV weather report in the comfort of his warm home. Now all he knew was he had never felt so raw and cold in his life, the blasting wind unyielding, blowing relentlessly with a horrible whistling sound. Soon his face felt numb and he took off his useless goggles and hung them round his neck, his eyes narrowed against the biting wind.

Slowly they struggled up the mountain which mocked them with false crests until the climb seemed endless. Luke remembered the myth about hell where someone was condemned to push a boulder up a mountain which always rolled backwards, eventually, carrying him down to start all over again.

The climb had now become so gruelling that Luke forgot about the wolves and Finn's delusions. All he could think of was how to keep himself going, plodding up the mountain, pushing his ski sticks into the soft snow, quite often sliding back so that he felt he was making no progress at all.

Nevertheless, after what seemed like an eternity, the trees began to thin out and they were out on the bare snow-covered slope, still plodding on, bent forwards into the full blast of the wind.

Then, quite suddenly, what Luke had thought was yet another false crest turned out to be the summit, and they were standing looking down at another densely forested valley.

A feeling of utter despair filled Luke.

"Don't say it." Finn's voice was thin and frail.

"Where's Rock?" Luke asked in a monotone.

"It should be there."

"But it's not. You've made a serious error of judgment, Finn. We shouldn't be going in this direction at all."

"That's impossible," said Finn doggedly.

"And you won't even admit it, like you won't even admit you're wrong about your brother." Luke spat out the venom, wanting to hurt as much as he could now.

"Shut up!" said Finn.

"You just won't admit you're wrong."

"I'm not."

"Your brother's dead. You got the direction wrong."

"No."

"Your brother's dead," repeated Luke viciously. "You got the direction wrong."

"Shut up!"

They were like two quarrelling kids in a playground, wanting to fight but too afraid, or maybe, in this case, just too exhausted.

"Rock *must* be in the next valley," muttered Finn. "I

underestimated the distance, that's all – not the direction."

"How do you work that out?"

"Because if we'd gone in the wrong direction, the mountains would have been higher and the valleys deeper."

"Let me see the map."

"You won't understand it." But Finn moved closer to show him, unfolding the air map with stiff, numb fingers. "Look at the size of the mountains." Luke felt a flash of reassurance, but it quickly burnt out. He glanced down at his watch to see that it was almost four and knew the light would be going very soon.

"So we'll camp in the valley," he stated flatly.

"We'll have to."

What about their fathers? thought Luke. All this waiting must be terrible for them - if they were still alive.

As they skied downhill, zigzagging amongst the monotony of the tall pines, Luke actually saw the pack padding down the valley, clearly visible for a moment through a gap in the trees. They were only there for an instant, dark shapes against the snow, and then they disappeared in the darkness, running in a line.

"What is it?" Finn had also stopped a few metres away.

"I saw the wolves – the whole pack."

"So?"

"They're stalking us."

But Finn shook his head. "You've failed to notice something important." His voice contained a note of triumph.

"What's that?"

"Where you saw your wolves—"

"They're not *my* wolves." Luke was indignant, as if Finn was accusing him of hallucinating.

"Never mind." Finn was immediately placating. "Don't get worked up all over again. Those wolves were running down a fire-break – a long slice of the forest where the trees have been felled. See, the gap is where the stumps have been buried under the snow."

"You mean—" Luke grappled with an impossible idea – one that contained hope – an emotion that had almost run out on him. "You mean we're near civilisation?"

"It can't be that far." Finn had repeated that phrase

so many times, but this time he might just be right.

Luke gave a great sigh of relief.

"You could have trusted me," Finn complained.

"I know. I'm sorry." And he was. "How far do you reckon we've got to go?"

"I'm not going to say the next valley," said Finn. "I could be wrong. But Rock can't be that far away now."

That phrase again, thought Luke, but he felt completely re-energised. As they began to zigzag on down through the dark pines, he called out over his shoulder, "I should have trusted you, Finn. I'm sorry."

They made camp around the base of a large pine, building up a fire and erecting the bivouac outside the tent and then moving inside as darkness fell.

"We'd better keep up the rationing," said Finn. "Just in case the airfield's another day's trek."

"Some people from the airport would have cut that fire-break, wouldn't they?" said Luke. "We must be getting near now."

"We need to be careful," replied Finn abruptly. "One can between us and we'll share an apple."

But Luke was starving. "Let's each have a whole

can." He was almost salivating at the very idea, salivating like a hungry wolf. "That'll leave us another one to share for breakfast and maybe that orange." The very thought of even half an orange made him heady with delight.

"No," said Finn.

Luke's temper, never far from the surface now, broke out of control again, despite the good news of the fire-break. Suddenly nothing mattered except food.

"For heaven's sake—"

"We've got to be careful," repeated Finn.

"*You* be careful. I won't."

"No way. We both do the same. We conserve."

Luke grabbed the torch from the floor of the tent and flashed the beam in Finn's face. He looked amazingly smug and Luke wanted to hit him. Instead he shone the torch straight into his eyes, as if he was about to interrogate him. "I want that can," he said.

"You get half." Finn was unmoved.

"I want the whole can and what's more I'm going to have it."

"I said, no."

"Who the hell do you think you are? No way are you

the leader round here."

"Listen, Luke." Finn spoke patiently, which only made Luke's temper soar to fresh heights. "We're not there yet."

"We *are* there. It's a day's skiing – maybe not even that. So give me the can." Luke realised that when they had repacked the backpacks that morning, Finn had taken the food while Luke had got the torch and water bottle. "Give me the can," he repeated, clenching his fist.

"I'll give you half."

"You'll give me the whole thing."

They had come to a total impasse as Luke blazed the torch into Finn's eyes again and Finn tried to protect them with shaking hands. Could he be afraid? wondered Luke. More triumph filled him. In the back of his mind he knew he was completely out of order, but all he could think of was the food. His basic instinct was to eat and stay alive. He *had* to have food.

Luke punched Finn hard on the arm.

"Get off!"

He punched him again and still Finn didn't retaliate.

"Do you want me to kill you?"

"No," said Finn. "I want you to leave me alone."

"Give me that can."

"No."

"Now!"

"It's still no."

Luke dropped the torch and dived for Finn's backpack, trying to pull at the straps while Finn held him off. Luke kicked out and Finn got him in a headlock. As he put the pressure on, Luke still tore at the straps, swearing and kicking, hardly able to believe what was happening, but needing food more than he had ever needed food before in his life.

Finn's headlock tightened. "Leave the bag."

"No way."

"You're going to get hurt."

"Try me."

Luke began to choke as the headlock tightened even more and he kicked out at Finn again and again, not sure how much contact he was making, but pleased at the odd grunt of pain.

Suddenly, the headlock loosened and with a cry of wild joy Luke managed to undo the straps of the backpack. He was just about to root inside when he felt

Finn let go completely as the tent filled with a bitter smell. Then there was a crackling and rustling sound and Finn began to yell.

Luke froze.

He couldn't turn round. He daren't turn round. But the smell grew stronger and again Finn yelled. The sound was terrible to hear.

Luke forced himself to turn round and saw that a dark sinewy shape had inserted itself between the bivouac and the open flap of the tent.

He was gazing at a young wolf.

Then Luke realised the wolf had sunk his teeth into Finn's flesh, its jaws locked around Finn's ankle. With a series of small, sharp, dragging movements, the wolf was trying to pull Finn out. As it did so, the wolf was snarling and yelping – and Luke could tell just how hungry he was.

Attack

Luke dithered, not knowing what to do. Finn's yells and the dreadful snarling of the wolf assaulted his ears.

At last Luke's frantic fingers grabbed one of the cans and he threw it at the wolf. But the blow was only glancing, and he knew he had to go for the creature's head – fast.

Half crouching in the confined space, Luke picked up the other can and hit the wolf hard on the head while Finn's yells reached a new height and the pack outside began to howl. The wolf yelped again and again, then, suddenly letting go of Finn's ankle, ran outside the tent, still yelping, and joined the dark shapes that were sitting in a half circle. Shivering violently, Luke gazed across at the wolf that had attacked them, a white streak in the fur above its eyes, conspicuous in the bright moonlight. Then he turned back to Finn.

Switching on the torch, Luke saw blood seeping through the leg of his cousin's torn ski pants.

He was no longer screaming, but whimpering with pain. "Have they gone?" he gasped.

"They're waiting outside."

"We shouldn't have let the fire go out."

"We were too tired," said Luke.

"I was a fool." Finn sobbed with pain. "I should have insisted we slept in shifts, took turns to keep a lookout – however tired we were."

Luke was shaking with the shock of it all as well as the fear of the wolves making a new attack. "Let me look at that bite."

Luke shifted position, glanced outside and saw that the wolves were still there, two of them licking the head of the young wolf he had injured. Now it was crouched down on the ground, whimpering.

Balancing the torch on the backpack, Luke pulled up the leg of Finn's ski pants – sticky with blood – to reveal a deep bite that showed the impression of the wolf's teeth. Digging in Finn's backpack, Luke pulled out the first-aid kit – some Band-Aid, a wad of cottonwool, a couple of rolls of bandage, a tube of antiseptic cream, some small safety-pins and a pair of scissors. He was pretty sure that while there might be enough supplies for the moment, they would soon run out – just like the food. How could he have been so selfish? He blamed himself bitterly for what had happened. If he hadn't been fighting for food they would have seen the wolf coming.

"What shall I do?" asked Luke.

"How deep is it?" Finn's voice came out of the darkness.

"Really deep."

"Then pull it together with something. What have you got?"

"Band-Aid."

"OK. Go ahead. Stop the bleeding."

Luke wiped the wound with antiseptic while Finn yelled with pain. "For goodness' sake, be careful!"

"I didn't mean to hurt you. Now what do I do?"

"Cut strips of Band-Aid and drag the edges of the wound together. Then cover the whole thing with a bandage and fasten it tightly."

"Will you be able to ski?"

"I'll have to. Go on – just do your best." Finn was sobbing with pain again as Luke went to work. "Where are the wolves?"

"Still outside."

"They could try again," said Finn in desperation.

"I thought you said they weren't hungry."

"I was wrong. I can be wrong. Like you."

Luke carried on, occasionally glancing outside. The wolves were still in a half circle and the one that he had attacked, with its distinctive white flash, now apparently recovered, was sitting with the others.

He finished winding a bandage as tightly as he could around Finn's ankle, pinning it together and pulling down the leg of his ski pants. Finn was quiet now, only occasionally giving out a gasp of pain.

"How does it feel?"

"Lousy."

"Are these painkillers?" Luke had found a bottle of pills in the first-aid kit.

"Yes, but they make you sleepy."

"That's what we're going to do. Sleep."

"Not with those wolves around. What are they doing now?"

Luke looked out. The wolves were gazing up at the moon. Then one of them got up on to all fours and then another and another. Slowly a different kind of howling began, each voice on a different note in a strange harmony that was almost a melody. Luke continued to watch silently until, as if at a pre-arranged signal, the wolves began to pad slowly away into the darkness.

"They've gone."

"They might come back."

"I'll keep watch," said Luke. "We'll eat more rations and then you must get some sleep. You're going to find the journey tough tomorrow."

"We'll take it in turns to keep watch. What's the time?"

"Just after midnight. And we're not taking turns. You'll need all the strength you can get tomorrow."

"So will you." Finn was reluctant to give in.

"But I wasn't bitten by a wolf."

"OK." Finn sighed. "But are you going to be able to keep awake?"

"Of course." Luke wasn't sure that he could, but was determined to try.

Suddenly a grim thought filtered into Luke's mind. Didn't Finn realise that what had just happened to him was what had happened to his brother? Except Karl *had* been dragged away. Then Luke realised that this was definitely not the time to remind him.

After they had eaten, Finn took a couple of the painkillers, and almost immediately fell into a deep sleep while Luke sat at the open flap of the tent, determined to stay awake. He kept his eyes fixed on the glade where the wolves had been, shivering in the freezing air. Luke wondered whether to relight the fire or not, and in the end decided to do so just to make sure he stayed awake.

Warily, still afraid the wolves might return, Luke gathered some twigs and then some bigger pieces of wood. He built the twigs into a miniature wigwam in the remains of the old fire, and taking care to conserve the matches, he tried to light the twigs.

But they were too damp and he cursed himself for being so stupid and inexperienced. Then he hunted in his backpack for paper and found a bag that had originally contained the much fought over tins, and another, larger bag that had once held the apples.

Carefully tearing a tiny strip from each of the bags, Luke inserted them into the middle of the twig wigwam and struck yet another of the precious matches. He had to use several of them before the twigs caught, smoking at first. Then, using his torch, Luke found some more dry twigs which had been protected from the snow under a pine.

Hurriedly he grabbed as many as he could and carefully piled them on top of his tiny flame. One of them caught and then another, until he had achieved a miniature fire which he managed to feed, frequently dashing back to the trees for more dry twigs, afraid that the wolves would leap out of the undergrowth at any moment.

So he could carry more twigs at one go and not have to go out into the darkness so often, Luke emptied out his rucksack and crammed the twigs into it. Eventually he was able to gaze in some satisfaction at his much bigger fire on which he began to carefully place even larger pieces of wood until the blaze was crackling away.

We should have kept it going, he thought. Then the wolves wouldn't have attacked.

Still keeping a sharp lookout for the wolves, Luke went out into the darkness and foraged for even bigger pieces of wood, searching under the pines, getting as much material as he possibly could and bringing the stuff back, stacking it near the heat so it would have a chance to dry.

Then, when he had built up a large pile of wood, he sat down and checked his watch. It was half past three in the morning and he was so pleased with the success of his fire that he didn't feel tired at all. Sitting with his sleeping bag tucked round him, Luke stared deep into the flames, watching the sparks fly and the wood spitting and crackling.

Warm and relaxed after his exertions, exhaustion descended on him without warning like a soft blanket and his head began to nod. He forced his eyes open and then staggered to his feet, prowling round the fire, but he soon found that he was practically asleep on the move. Gazing down at the snowy ground, Luke again saw it as the most wonderfully tempting blanket and he sank to his knees by the fire, struggling into his sleeping bag again, his eyes closing as he pitched forward and fell into deep, deep sleep.

"Some lookout."

Luke slowly woke to find himself in a foetal position, curled up on the ground, his sleeping bag still around him, beside the dying embers of the fire.

"What?"

"I thought you were meant to be on guard duty, but you went to sleep instead."

Finn limped over to where Luke was still lying, but he was grinning and didn't look angry. He winced in pain several times, and Luke felt ashamed.

"I lit the fire. Then I was so tired that I had a bit of a sit down and that was it. I'm sorry."

"You did your best," said Finn. "Stop blaming yourself. You needed sleep, too."

"We could have been attacked again."

"Looks like it was a great fire," said Finn generously.

"Do you think the flames kept the wolves away?"

"Yes."

Luke yawned, feeling tense and very stiff. He had a throbbing headache, but Luke knew Finn must be feeling much worse with that deep bite in his ankle. "Do you want me to take a look at that—"

"No," interrupted Finn abruptly.

"The bite could be infected."

"I'd rather you left it alone."

"Does it hurt?"

"I can hack it." Finn looked away and Luke knew he was wondering if he could manage. But there was no other solution. Suddenly Luke had the terrifying thought that with Finn hurt, he might have to make the journey on his own.

"I can cope," Luke muttered. "If you want to stay here. If you can't ski—"

"Who said I wanted to do anything of the kind?" snapped Finn brusquely.

"I just thought—"

"Well, you thought wrong, didn't you? I'll be OK. With a bit of luck we should reach Rock by nightfall."

"And what if we don't?"

"Then we'll just have to keep going."

"What about breakfast?" asked Luke.

"Half a can each. Aren't you pleased you didn't—"

"OK, I was wrong and I'm sorry. I behaved like an idiot."

Finn gazed at him. "We all have to learn this stuff. OK, maybe you were selfish over the food, but you didn't chicken out when the wolf attacked me. Your quick-thinking saved my life. Again. Isn't it time I saved yours?"

"Let's hope you don't get the chance."

"Thanks."

"You know what I mean. I just don't want any more trouble, that's all."

"I can't guarantee a problem-free journey." Finn paused. "I was thinking about my dad – and yours," he added.

"They've got food – more food than we have. And my dad can move around – he'll help to look after Brett." Luke tried to be comforting.

"Sure." Finn nodded. "They'll be fine."

But they both knew they were just trying to convince each other.

*

Finn pulled his boot over his injured ankle with some care, and flinched.

"How does it feel?" asked Luke.

"Lousy."

They looked up at the sky which was heavily overcast, with snowflakes already drifting down.

"Is there going to be another snowstorm?" asked Luke.

"There's no wind. But I reckon we could have a steady snowfall."

"The wolves—"

Finn cut Luke off abruptly. "I told you, normally the wolves are shy creatures. They don't usually attack humans."

"Unless they're desperate," said Luke. "And right now they seem very hungry indeed. So what are they going to do? Hunt us down?"

"That attack last night was made by a young wolf. It was inexperienced. It hadn't learnt to hunt properly, otherwise it wouldn't have tried to take me on."

"He hunted you pretty effectively though!"

Finn only shrugged and stepped on to his skis.

As he pulled on his skins, amazed at the way the silicon adhesive could be reused time and time again, Luke decided to take yet another risk. Had Finn missed the irony of the attack by a young wolf? "Do you still think Karl's out here somewhere?"

"His body was never found."

"You still think he's alive?"

"I've *got* to think he's alive. Everyone keeps telling me he's dead."

This was the frankest admission that Finn had made and Luke knew he would have to tread carefully. But even so something made him press on. Somehow he felt this was the right moment.

"Could you bear it if he *was* dead?"

"No. We were close – really close." For the first time, Finn didn't seem angry, he was just trying to be honest. Finn paused, and then said quietly, "I don't know what to believe. They never found his body," he repeated like a litany. "That's something, isn't it?"

Luke didn't reply. He didn't want to provide a neat wrap-up to their conversation. Better to leave it all up in the air, he thought. After all, wasn't that what Finn wanted?

*

They spent the next two hours plodding up the much steeper side of the mountain which turned out to be the most exhausting climb of the last two days. Snow fell, softly and lightly, and a wind blew up, gently at first and then more strongly, gradually becoming bitterly cold.

As Finn stopped to check the compass Luke came alongside him.

"How's your ankle?"

Finn ignored him, although Luke could see the pain in his eyes. "The snow's getting thicker and we could have a white-out, so I've got to keep looking at the compass to check that we're staying on course."

"How much longer do we have to climb?"

"Another couple of hours – at least."

Luke felt instantly depressed and then remembered Finn's ankle. If he was finding the going hard, then it must be hell for his cousin. Suddenly Luke felt a rush of elation. To form a relationship with Finn had been difficult, but Luke felt that he had finally won his colours. They were real friends now because they had faced so much adversity together.

Then his optimism disappeared as he sensed they were being followed. He kept stopping and looking round, convinced that the wolves were keeping pace with them, waiting for an opportunity, and gradually Luke began to fall behind.

"Hang on," he called to Finn. "We must keep together."

"Well, get on with it then," said Finn impatiently, pushing himself to the limit, his face screwed up in pain.

"If you want I could fix you another bandage."

"Shut up and keep going," was the only reply he received.

They started off again and had been climbing for about forty minutes when Luke saw movement in the trees some metres away and came to an immediate halt. Finn, who was keeping pace with him, did the same.

"What is it?"

"In the trees. Look—"

There were definitely wolf-like shapes in the semi-darkness of the forest. "The pack," Finn muttered.

"Are they trailing us?"

"They could be – or this might be one of their regular routes. They're pretty territorial and constantly patrol their boundaries."

Luke hoped Finn was right. Privately he suspected the pack was playing some lethal game with them and would soon be moving in for the kill.

When they were halfway up the mountain, Luke's exhaustion suddenly overtook him and his body felt so heavy that it was as if he was dragging along a huge sack full of lead. His backpack had rubbed one of his shoulders, making the skin incredibly sore, and the bitter cold had chafed his face until his lips were chapped and bleeding.

The trees were thinning out now and there was no shelter. As if to round off the torture, the freezing wind was full of snow flurries which seemed to be hurling themselves straight into his face.

Finn, however, was making good progress despite the wound on his ankle, and Luke felt admiration for him.

"You've got to keep moving," said Finn sharply.

"I'm trying to."

"Rock could be in the next valley."

"So you said before."

"We don't want to spend another night on the mountain. Not with a pack of hungry wolves."

"I'm trying."

"You're not trying hard enough."

Luke bent forward in the wind and struggled on, his face taking the full onslaught of the bitter wind.

"You're not going fast enough!" shouted Finn.

"Go to hell!"

"That's where we're gonna be if you don't go a lot faster."

The trees had almost entirely thinned out now and they were out on the bare mountain. Here the snow was deep and treacherous and they sank in on every step.

"Go for it!" yelled Finn.

"I have to take a rest," barked Luke. He stopped, pulling off his backpack to ease his sore shoulder.

"I'll get you moving if it's the last thing—"

As Finn spoke, the snow gave way and Luke disappeared.

Cavern

Luke landed on his back with a thud that knocked all the breath out of him, staring up at the grey and overcast sky above. He rolled over to one side and found he was lying on a pile of soft snow in a luminous cavern that looked as if it was made of crystal, shimmering a deep meridian blue with a touch of translucent green.

Relieved that he was unhurt, Luke lay there, amazed to find he still had his rucksack in his hand, but when he removed his skis and tried to get to his feet, the snow was so soft and so deep that he found himself up to his knees in the stuff. Terrified he might lose his skis and sticks, Luke clutched them tightly while clumsily working on his rucksack again, sweating with the effort, despite the cold.

Panic set in as he gazed at the sheer walls of the ice cavern and then he saw Finn gazing down at him through the hole in the roof of the cavern.

"You OK?" Finn asked coolly, as if nothing much had happened.

"I'm not hurt – at least I don't think I am – but I can't get out. The walls are too sheer. What am I going to do?"

"We'll think of something," said Finn.

"You'll have to think of something fast." Luke was shaking as he tried to move forward, finding he was sinking deeper into the snow. Determined not to give up, Luke struggled on until suddenly he felt rock beneath his feet. Pushing himself forward, Luke found himself on rising ground and eventually managed to stand free, stamping the snow off his legs.

"You still OK?" called Finn.

"I've found a bit of firm ground – but how do I get out?"

"That's what I was wondering." Finn sounded

ludicrously casual.

Panic swept Luke yet again as he stared at the ice-smooth walls of the cavern. He moved forward again to see if he could spot anywhere that could give him a foothold to climb out, and slipped, cracking his head against a snow-covered rock.

Luke came to, lying on his stomach, staring down into a cavity that looked like a long, dark tunnel. He scrabbled in the pocket of his skisuit and wrenched out the torch, glad to see it was still in one piece.

Luke gave a choked cry of triumph as the beam swept the tunnel. At least he could see what he was doing.

Then he heard a shout from above and the sound of a small object clunking against the ice.

Again Finn's head appeared. "The compass... I dropped the compass, trying to find a new bandage."

Luke checked and found the compass, but the dial was broken. Disaster had struck again. Now they wouldn't know what direction to take.

"The wound – it's bad. It's started to bleed again."

"And I can't get out." Luke gave a hysterical laugh,

but actually he felt more like crying. "It looks like there's a tunnel down here, but I daren't go down it. I mean — I might never come out again."

"You will," said Finn with his usual confidence. "It's bound to come out somewhere. Is the tunnel going up or down?"

"Up. I think."

"You got the torch?"

"Yes."

"Go up a little way and see where the tunnel goes. You've got nothing to lose. You can always come back again." Finn suddenly sounded much weaker.

"I thought you said you'd work out a way to get me out."

"Well, I can't. Try the tunnel." Finn sounded drained.

Luke shoved the broken compass into his jacket pocket. Maybe Finn could repair the thing.

"I'm sorry," said Finn.

"What about?"

"The compass."

"Don't worry about me then."

"I am."

"I won't even know—" Then Luke broke off as a young grey wolf emerged panting from the tunnel, fur bristling, snout wrinkled back into a snarl.

Luke stared at the creature in disbelief.

"Oh, God," he breathed.

"What's going on?" yelled Finn.

"Keep your voice down," hissed Luke.

"Why?"

"There's a wolf."

"*What?*"

"There's a wolf."

"Where?"

"Down here. With me. Now shut up."

The silence from above was so dense Luke could almost feel a wall between him and Finn.

The wolf gazed at him steadily.

Luke didn't dare to even blink. His heart was hammering and his throat was so dry he could hardly breathe.

The wolf stared back at him, suddenly moving into a crouching position, as if about to spring.

Luke gazed back and their eyes locked.

Slowly the wolf began to growl and he could see a slither of saliva form in the corner of its mouth.

Still they gazed into each other's eyes.

Then the wolf began to move towards him.

Luke looked round for a weapon, and then realised he had the torch. He raised it above his head and the wolf seemed to hesitate.

Gathering a little confidence, Luke waved the torch about in a wide arc. Then he switched it off and on again in rapid succession, shining the beam directly into the creature's eyes.

The wolf began to snarl.

Luke shone the torch in the wolf's eyes again, this time daring to get nearer to it, making the light more dazzling.

Suddenly the young wolf turned round and began to run away, its fur seeming to shimmer in the torchlight.

Luke could hardly believe his good luck. Somehow he had scared the thing away. But would it come back?

He waited, nerves screaming, hardly able to breathe.

But seconds and then minutes ticked past and the

wolf didn't return.

Slowly, very slowly, Luke began to relax a little.

Then he had a terrible thought.

His only possible means of escape was through the tunnel where the wolf could be waiting in the dark. Luke then looked at the torch and realised the beam was not nearly so sharp. The batteries were running down.

"Luke," hissed Finn from above.

"What is it?"

"Where's the wolf?"

"Gone."

"Thanks for telling me."

"It's gone down the tunnel. Where I've got to go."

"If you meet the wolf in the tunnel," advised Finn, "shine the torch beam in its eyes."

"Brilliant. That's what I've *been* doing. But now the batteries are running down. The torch'll be dead soon," he muttered, a wave of panic surging through him.

"I've got some spare batteries."

Luke felt a flicker of hope.

"Hang on." Finn was clearly foraging in his

backpack. "Here we are. Now catch! If you miss these two, we haven't got any more."

"Wait! Let me get into position."

"Hurry up. I feel lousy."

"What sort of lousy?"

"Dizzy."

"What about the bleeding? Has it stopped?"

"No."

"Put that bandage on."

"Catch these first."

Leaving his skis and sticks, Luke struggled into the deep snow until he was standing directly under the hole. "Come on then," he yelled, cupping his hands and catching the two batteries, one after the other. He slipped and fell over in the soft snow, still gripping the batteries and holding them high in the air as if they were an offering to the gods.

Luke picked himself up, still firmly clutching the batteries, and hauled himself back on to the rock, away from the softness below. He then fitted the batteries into the torch and threw the old ones away. "OK," he said. "I'll go for the tunnel."

"You'll come out higher up the mountain,"

said Finn.

"Have you seen a wolf up there?"

"I haven't seen it."

"So it's waiting for me?"

There was no reply from Finn, so Luke answered the question himself.

"We'll soon find out," he said unhappily.

Luke ducked down, his rucksack hitting the roof of the tunnel, making him bend down even lower. Shining the bright beam he saw that the tunnel seemed to be some kind of ice-covered fissure in the rock with a glassy, slippery floor.

The wolf could be lurking round any corner.

Luke sniffed, wondering if he would pick up the wolves' sour smell, but there was nothing on the air.

Cautiously he inched his way round the bend and found a long passage of ice disappearing into darkness. Luke clambered on, heart hammering, sure he was about to meet the wolf again.

The torch picked out the blue-green ice of the walls of the tunnel as he wound his way up, feeling increasing tension at each bend. Then, suddenly, Luke found the fissure was going down – so steeply that he began to slide, holding himself and the torch up as best he could.

He managed to come to a halt, gazing down hopelessly, wondering if he was going to become trapped somewhere deep in a mountain labyrinth for ever. Then, without further hesitation, he sat down and slid on, suspecting this was the most foolish move he could make. But what else could he do?

Fortunately, he didn't slide far, and to his joy the tunnel began to ascend again, this time much more steeply.

Luke tried to climb, seriously impeded by having to carry his skis, sticks and the torch. He hacked away at the ice with his heel until he managed to make a foothold, and slowly and painfully was able to move forward a notch. Once he slid down again and then, with an enormous effort, managed to push himself on, despite the skis and sticks he was carrying.

Soon, the tunnel began to narrow, but Luke carried on, flashing his torch ahead, still climbing as the narrow space became slightly wider and less steep.

Suddenly Luke felt a darting breeze wafting down

the tunnel. Was he getting somewhere at last? The sharp breeze must surely mean he was coming out into the open air. Then he smelt something else that was familiar. He paused, a thrill of horror stirring deep inside him. How could he forget that familiar smell? It was the pungent scent of a wolf.

Pack

Too afraid to continue, Luke waited, listening intently. Where was it? Where was the wolf?

Then he heard a scrabbling, sliding sound. Was the wolf as afraid of him as he was of it?

Luke switched off the torch and waited. The scrabbling came again. With sudden decision, Luke forced himself to make a move and rounded the corner, still with his burden of sticks and skis. Raw fear surged through him, his heart pounding so hard that his chest hurt. Then he suddenly switched the torch on and its sharp beam picked out the young wolf, crouched, with some kind of small rodent between its paws.

Luke felt sick, but he stood his ground, shining the torch beam into the wolf's eyes. The creature snarled and then abruptly turned away, still with the rodent in its mouth, scurrying up the tunnel. As the wolf made its escape, Luke thought he could see a trace, just a glimmer, of distant light.

Luke's hopes soared and he felt almost delirious with elation. He climbed on, the slope much more gentle now and the roof higher, the pinpoint of light getting bigger and brighter all the time.

Then dark shadows filled the hole in the snow and Luke came to a halt.

The young wolf was staring down at him intently. So were the rest of the pack.

Terrified, Luke flashed his torch up at them and heard a muted snarl, but none of the wolves moved back. Slowly he realised how stupid he was being. The beam wouldn't agitate the pack because all they could see was a faint light that roused their curiosity, but not their fear. Luke tried to think clearly and to fight off the panic that was beginning to fill him.

He focused his thoughts on Finn, alone and wounded on the mountainside. Suppose the pack had already killed him and was now waiting for their second victim of the morning?

Luke had never felt such defeat. They had battled against the wild and lost. But what possible chance had they had in the first place? The odds against them had always been overwhelming and the presence of the pack was the last card the wild had to play. They were going to die and, as a result, so were Dad and Brett.

Luke waited. Would the pack come for him? Or should he climb up to them? Seven pairs of eyes seemed fixed on him, hungry and determined.

Then, as suddenly as they had appeared, the pack withdrew, leaving only the young wolf. Had he been left to guard the opening? Had the pack already feasted off Finn?

Then the young wolf lowered his head, sniffed the air and suddenly bounded away, leaving Luke to gaze up at the misty orange blob that was the sun breaking through the clouds.

The climb up to the mouth of the tunnel was steep but easy, and as he pushed himself on Luke wondered, over and over again, what had happened to Finn. Slowly, unwillingly, he became increasingly convinced he must be dead.

Trying to prepare himself, Luke clambered out of the crevasse, immediately finding himself in deep snow, much further up the mountain than he had imagined.

In trepidation, he looked round for Finn's body, or the tell-tale remains of his kit in the snow.

Then to his enormous relief Luke saw Finn, further down the slope, still wearing his rucksack. He seemed to be making something in the snow. Then, to Luke's amazement, he realised Finn was building a snowman.

A wave of indignation swept Luke. How could Finn be doing something so ludicrous as building a snowman while he, Luke, had been running the risk of being eaten? Had Finn finally gone completely crazy?

The sun was higher in the sky, shining brightly, making the snow glisten.

He looked at his watch. It was just after midday.

Then he saw that Finn was now sitting in the snow,

staring ahead. A dreadful chill embraced Luke which had nothing to do with the freezing conditions. Now what was he going to do? This was almost as bad as falling into the crevasse. Finn looked as if he was no longer able to cope.

"Finn!" Luke yelled. "What are you *doing*?"

Luke waded through the snow to Finn, staring into his blank eyes, realising his ski pants were covered in fresh blood at the ankle.

"You're bleeding."

Finn looked down at his leg in surprise. "I don't know what happened," he said.

"You got attacked last night – by a wolf." Luke gazed past Finn and saw a circle of paw prints in the snow.

"Did they hurt you again?"

"Who?"

"The wolves."

"I saw Karl. He's the one with the blue eyes," said Finn, staring at Luke as if he had never seen him before, as if Luke was a complete stranger. "Now he's a wolf, he can run faster than ever. I couldn't catch him. No one could catch him."

Luke didn't know what to do. He had no idea how to handle a situation like this. Was Finn in shock, or had the loss of blood and his infected wound made him delirious?

"We have to reach Rock. I need you, Finn," Luke pleaded, desperate for him to regain control. "You've got the expertise. Your father – my father – they're both trapped in the plane. The plane crashed – remember? If we don't get to Rock and organise a rescue, they're going to die. Don't you understand, Finn – your father could die if we don't reach Rock. You can't waste time with a snowman."

Finn gazed at him in bewilderment. He didn't seem to have taken in a word Luke had said. Maybe it's not shock, he thought. Could he be suffering from exposure? Now he was beginning to despair of ever reaching the real Finn again.

"We've got to get going."

"Karl's fine. He's running with the pack."

"OK, but your dad's not fine at all. He's in a lot of pain and he needs help. Like now!"

Finn stared at him and then got to his feet, shaking his head as if he didn't know where he was.

Then, driven by sudden instinct, Luke grabbed Finn's shoulder, swung him round and slapped his cousin across the face as hard as he could.

Caught off balance, Finn fell backwards into the snow with a howl of pain, not from the slapping, Luke was sure, but from the wound in his ankle as he made contact with the ground. More blood welled out, staining the brilliant whiteness of the snow.

"Let me fix that," said Luke, hurrying warily towards him, but Finn didn't offer any resistance. Instead he lay still, eyes closed, lips working but no sound coming out.

Both their backpacks were lying in the snow and Luke realised Finn must have somehow managed to bring his up the mountain as well. Rummaging in Finn's he dragged out what remained of the first-aid kit and then sat down in the snow beside Finn.

"I'm going to re-bandage the wound on your ankle," he said, with as much authority as he could muster.

Still Finn said nothing, lying on his back with his eyes closed.

"We're being guided," he said as Luke pulled up the leg of his ski pants.

"Who by?"

"Karl. He wants to get us through to Rock."

Luke pulled off the old bandage, making Finn cry out in pain. He was obviously incapable of rational thought at the moment, so as Luke worked on the new bandage he decided all he could do was to go along with Finn's delusions and not to argue with him.

Luke gazed down at the gaping wound which now had a yellowish glaze on it. The sight confirmed Luke's fears. It's infected, he thought miserably. Luke placed a hand on Finn's forehead, which was hot and sweaty.

He wiped the infected area with antiseptic cream and pulled the ragged tear together again with fresh strips of Band-Aid. Finn didn't cry out this time, but he winced with the pain, his face white and strained.

"We'll have to get going." Luke wound the new bandage round Finn's ankle and pinned the ends fast.

"Is Rock far away?" he asked.

"Not very."

Luke helped Finn stagger to his feet, realising that he was very much on his own.

They both looked up at the sky, only to see the sun disappearing behind a bank of swollen clouds.

"The weather's breaking up," said Luke. "Do you

think we're in for more snow?"

"Could be." Suddenly, Finn seemed to have snapped back to normality. The change was amazingly fast. But how long would it last?

Luke realised there was no way of telling. "So what do we do?" he asked, trying to sound as despondent as possible so that Finn would take the lead.

"Go up the mountain and down the other side." Finn made the process sound simple.

"Will Rock be there?"

"Karl said there's more mountains in the way."

Luke's heart sank. Finn was still labouring under his delusions. For now, there was only one thing they *could* do. Go up the mountain and down the other side and if the airfield was in the next valley then they would have, at last, reached their goal. But if Rock wasn't there, Luke began to doubt if he could get Finn any further. His ankle was poisoned and soon they would both die of exposure, and their fathers too.

As if to underline their fate, more snowflakes began to fall, coming down faster and more thickly than before, and within a minute or so they were in a white-out again.

Raw

"What shall we do?" Luke was beginning to realise there could be a way through to the real Finn, bypassing the self-delusion. The more he could keep him in the present, the more Luke showed how much he relied on Finn, the more successful he might be, and, after all, success was survival.

"We must push on." Finn was decisive and realistic. "There's no shelter here. We need to be in the lee of the mountain and that means getting over the summit and at least some of the way down the other side. We could freeze to death up here. We *have* to keep moving." He paused. "This ankle really hurts. If I'm going to make it, I need to carry on now before it really stiffens up."

Amazingly, Finn seemed to have once again broken out of his delirium and Luke knew it was essential to capitalise on any moments of lucidity.

"OK," he said. "Let's go for it."

Head down, battling against the steadily falling snow, Luke was alarmed to find a wind was also getting up. Leaning on their ski sticks, they both attempted to get a grip with their skin-covered skis on the deepening snow. How far did they have to go? wondered Luke. He gazed up towards the summit of the mountain. He had taken off his goggles which had iced up yet again, but could still see nothing through the snowflakes. Panic swept him. His legs were leaden and his will to keep going was diminishing, replaced by a feeling of utter helplessness. Surely the summit couldn't be that far off? They seemed to have been climbing this mountain for a very long time. Luke felt as if he'd been wading through the snow for ever and could hardly bear to continue. The cold was another factor, and his face, the only exposed part of his body, seemed to be frozen solid, his lips cracked and sore, the snow driving against his eyes so that he was almost blinded.

Finn had moved into the lead now, and despite the pain of his ankle seemed to be pushing himself harder than ever, forging ahead without looking back.

Luke suddenly felt incredibly weak and his energy level dipped, falling away to almost nothing. He wanted to stop struggling on and lie down in the snow, which looked warm and inviting, a great white blanket beneath his feet.

He staggered and nearly fell, his ski sticks stuck in the snow, the weakness overpowering, the need to stop and sleep and forget everything paramount in his mind.

"What are you doing?" came Finn's all too familiar critical voice.

"I can't go on."

"You must." Finn kicked snow in Luke's face. "You know you've got to. Get up and get on with it." Now their roles were reversed and it was Finn who'd got a grip, and Luke who hadn't.

"I want to sleep."

"Get up!" yelled Finn against the wind. "We're almost at the summit." He was a bit more encouraging.

"How long?"

"Ten minutes."

"You're lying."

"Why should I?"

Luke dragged himself slowly and suspiciously to his feet. "*Are* you lying?"

"The summit's about ten minutes away. See for yourself."

Luke began to take some staggering steps forward. "You're making it up."

"Come and see for yourself," Finn repeated wearily, still shouting above the wind, hard, realistic, focused.

Luke did as he was told, head down, every step a huge effort, as if he was literally pulling himself along like a ton weight.

"Come on," said Finn encouragingly. "You can make it. You've *got* to make it."

His face raw in the freezing wind, Luke kept plodding on. He'd lost all track of time, lost even the sensation of moving forwards, as if he was walking on the spot and making no progress. The feeling seemed to go on a long time, until Finn's voice broke into his numbed thoughts.

"We're here. Can't you see? We're here!"

Luke gazed round him. Amazingly they had arrived on a broad summit that was littered with rocky outcrops, but where the density of the snowfall had brought visibility down to a few metres.

He began to stagger across the summit in the vain hope he could see into the valley below. But all vision was lost in swirling clouds of snow. Was Rock hidden in the white-out? Or was there just another forested valley? After all they'd been through, the frustration of not knowing was too much to bear. Then the howling began.

"No," Luke blurted out. "Not them as well. Please, God, not the pack. Not up here!"

Finn stood silently beside him, gazing at the snow clouds, seeming not to hear the howling at all, which Luke was sure was coming nearer.

"What are we going to do?" he demanded of his now silent companion. But Finn made no reply.

Then the pack appeared out of the snowstorm,

loping up the slope he and Finn had so painfully climbed, six fully grown adults and a young wolf following behind, their eyes staring ahead, seeming to take no interest whatever in Finn and Luke, running through the rocks, heading down the other side of the mountain.

The young wolf was the last to disappear into the white-out.

"They're showing us the way," said Finn.

"Don't talk rubbish," snapped Luke, unable to take any more.

But Finn was no longer labouring under delusion. "I've told you before, they've got their paths – like territorial boundaries—" Finn paused. "That's why they were howling just now – to lay claim to their territory. Rock could represent a potential food source, couldn't it? Wolves are known for being scavengers."

Luke shrugged and then said, "Maybe you're right. Perhaps they *are* showing us the way."

He suddenly felt light-headed, no longer capable of coherent thought.

"Or maybe they're going to ambush us," he said, reverting to his natural suspicions.

"Their minds don't work like that," replied Finn authoritatively. He was still sweating. "If they were going to attack, they'd have gone for us just now. I expect the airfield has plenty of dustbins, and the pack know that."

Luke felt a sudden spark of hope rising from his despair. "Are we going to follow them?" he asked.

"You bet we are," said Finn. "I always told you we'd be guided."

Unhooking and folding their skins yet again, they skied downhill, zigzagging slowly and purposefully, hearing the odd howl from the wolves, but the sounds seemed to be coming from much deeper in the valley.

Luke still couldn't see anything through the white-out, but the flakes seemed to be falling more gently. They were either sheltered from the wind or it was dropping.

Finn was skiing alongside him now, and Luke could just make out his strained sweating face and hear an occasional little grunt of pain. Checking the leg of Finn's ski pants, Luke saw that fresh blood was running on to his ski boot and leaving a blood trail in the snow.

"Stop!" he yelled. "You're bleeding again."

"Too bad," shouted back Finn.

"You're losing a lot of blood."

"We'll be in Rock soon."

"Will we?" Luke was still doubtful.

A faint orange blob appeared in the sky above them and the snowflakes lessened as they skied on until they came to a thin tree-line.

Beyond the pines were stumps and Luke felt another surge of hope.

"They've felled the trees," he shouted at Finn.

"Yes," he shouted back. "I didn't think they felled themselves."

"You reckon it's another firebreak?"

"I don't think so," Finn bawled back at him. "It's so the runway can be seen by the pilots."

More hope filled Luke. Could Finn be right? Were they really skiing towards safety at last? A pressing sense of urgency filled him. They had to raise the alarm. They had to get help.

As they skied on, the snow clouds slowly began to part and the cold sun came through.

But Luke still couldn't see the valley floor – and until

he did he wasn't going to let himself believe that Rock was there.

Then Finn stopped and raised a hand.

The sound of howling could distinctly be heard and to Luke's acute unease, it was much nearer.

Panic-striken, Luke and Finn increased their speed until suddenly, to their intense relief, a wooden cabin loomed up ahead of them. Luke felt almost delirious with joy at the sight of the simple structure. Surely that proved human habitation was near?

Then Finn whispered, "Don't move!"

To Luke's considerable disquiet he saw the pack had their heads in an upturned dustbin, paws scrabbling at the contents, while the young wolf, pushed aside, was howling piteously.

The pack was too preoccupied to pick up the boys' scent. Looking for cover, Luke saw a stack of oil drums to the left of the cabin. Signalling to Finn, very slowly and gently he began to ski towards them.

Finn followed him, taking a sideways glance every so often, but the wolves were still too busy to take any notice at all.

*

From the shelter of the oil drums Luke and Finn watched the wolves scavenging. They had only found a few tins that had some scraps left in them. At the moment, the pack were scouring them avidly with their tongues, but would that be enough to satisfy their appetites? wondered Luke. How hungry were they? But he knew the answer. The pack must be very hungry indeed.

After a while one of the larger wolves moved aside and allowed the young wolf to lick at a tin and Luke wondered if she was its mother.

Gazing down at Finn's ankle, Luke saw more blood was oozing out and realised the odds were still against them, even if they were really arriving at the last stage of this arduous journey. If the pack picked up their scent out here in the open, they'd be vulnerable to an attack.

Luke also knew that although he and Finn were equals now and knew each other's strengths and weaknesses, Finn was on burn-out, both mentally and physically, and Luke felt very much the same.

"Let's try and get past the pack," hissed Luke.

"While they're still scavenging."

"OK." But Finn's brow was shining with droplets of sweat, and Luke wondered if he could make it.

Then, suddenly, through another break in the trees, the clouds lifted again and Luke glimpsed the valley floor. Slowly the runway came into view and he gripped Finn's arm in disbelief. They'd made it. In spite of everything, they'd actually made it. There in front of them was an airfield, a runway, a control tower and a hangar. But where was the cafe with the Coca-Cola sign? Then Luke remembered that the cafe had just been a fantasy, a figment of his imagination. To him it had been so real and now Luke saw how easily acute stress altered the mind and substituted delusion for reality. This was what must have happened to Finn. Luke could understand it more clearly now.

Luke continued to gaze down at the airfield as if it was a mirage in the desert that might suddenly and mockingly disappear.

But it didn't. They had arrived at Rock. Then Luke realised with a chill of horror that there was a wolf pack between them and safety. A hungry wolf pack.

*

"Don't make a sound," whispered Finn. "The wolves have an acute sense of smell." He was back to normal again.

Luke nodded.

"What we have to do is to get away from the pack as fast as we can and make Rock before they catch on. As soon as we start moving, we're a potential target."

Luke glanced down at his watch and saw that it was just before two in the afternoon, and they had only limited time before sunset. He gazed at the gentle slope which led down to the valley. They wouldn't get up much speed on that and if the wolves decided to go for the kill they were finished. All they could do was try – there was no other alternative.

"Wait for my signal," whispered Finn.

Why don't we go now? wondered Luke – while the pack was still rooting about in another dustbin they seemed to have dragged out of a shattered wooden compound. Had they broken their way in? Or had the force of the snow done that for them?

"Let's go," hissed Luke.

"Wait."

One of the larger wolves had stepped back from the

dustbin and begun to howl. Slowly, one by one, the rest of the pack left their scavenging and stood back, joining in the howling which acquired a strange rhythm of its own. Each wolf picked up a separate note and Luke once again listened to the most mysterious, most chilling song he had ever heard. He glanced at Finn and saw he was staring at the young wolf as it joined in. As he did so, the rest of the pack fell silent and his single voice became a solo. Eventually the young wolf came to a stop and then, as if at an unseen signal, the pack returned to their scavenging.

"Now," said Finn, and propelling himself with his ski sticks, launched himself at the gentle snow-bound slope down the valley to Rock.

Luke followed, pushing on his sticks with all his strength. He looked back and almost fell, regaining his balance but realising he'd have to be careful. Fortunately, the wolves were still rooting in the dustbin and didn't look up. Were he and Finn safe? Luke prayed they were. He increased his speed, trying to catch up with Finn and put as much space between him and the pack as he could. Every moment counted.

Then, to his horror, Luke suddenly heard a yelping

and turned to look round again. Racing along at an incredible speed, the pack was in pursuit, and beginning to catch them up. Their sinewy legs pounded the snow and looking back yet again Luke saw the distance was narrowing still faster.

"They're after us!" he yelled at Finn, who had not glanced back at all. But he began to speed up immediately, head down, his skis creating a blur of snow.

A feeling of hopelessness overcame Luke as he imagined the wolves' teeth tearing at his flesh, penetrating bone. Now he would be the victim. The hunted. The kill.

Luke turned to gaze back again and saw the pack were even nearer. Losing concentration in his panic he lost his balance, rolling over in the snow, his skis high in the air.

The wolves charged towards him, jaws open to reveal the sharp teeth, salivating and coming in for the kill.

Gasping with shock, Luke tried to struggle to his feet. He half saw Finn turn and begin to ski back towards him, eyes full of despair.

Luke's panic was so great that he failed to hear the chattering sound in the air above him, although he could see Finn gaze up and, for some mad reason, stand still and stare at the sky.

Luke looked back again, sure the pack would soon be jumping at his throat. But they had also come to a halt, gazing up at the sky.

Luke dragged his eyes away from the pack and saw the helicopter circling above them, getting lower all the time. The wolves began to howl and then to turn away from this threateningly huge bird and head back up the hill, towards the remote forest and safety.

Luke laughed in triumph, hardly able to believe in his good fortune. Meanwhile, as the helicopter hovered not far above them, someone began to address them over an amplified loud hailer.

"Take off your skis and be ready to board! I repeat – take off your skis and be ready to board."

Luke and Finn released their skis and then saw a line being winched down with a harness on the end.

"OK," came the voice again. "One at a time."

A man was leaning out of the helicopter hatch dressed in paramedic uniform.

Finn went first, wincing as he put his weight on his ankle, clipping on the harness and then being pulled up into the helicopter. Luke waited for the harness to descend again and then clipped himself in. As he was winched up, the shock of nearly being devoured by the wolves hit him, and his whole body began to tremble.

In seconds he was inside the helicopter and had, at last, left the wilderness behind. The wild had reluctantly given them up.

Rescue

The pilot and paramedic introduced themselves as Don Parker and Steve Hanson. As they rose further from the ground, Luke closed his eyes against the appalling memory of the wolves and then opened them again, unable to believe they were safe at last. Then he remembered Finn's wounded ankle.

"He's got a bad gash in his leg. Finn got bitten by a wolf." Luke's voice was shaking badly and he could hardly get the words out. "And now I reckon he's got a fever."

"You from the Cessna?" asked Steve Hanson, the paramedic.

"Yes." Finn sounded faint, hesitant, suffering the same aftershock as Luke.

"The conditions have been appalling," said Don, shouting above the noise of the rotors. "So many white-outs that we haven't been able to fly."

"We can show you where the Cessna is," said Finn. "Our dads are hurt bad. Can we go there now?"

"Let's do that."

As the helicopter banked away from Rock and headed towards the mountains, Luke caught a glimpse of the pack running over the snow, the young wolf bounding ahead.

Finn gave the directions to Don as they flew over the summit and forested valley. Soon the raging torrent of the river and the broken bridge came into view.

"How did you get over that lot?" shouted Steve.

"The bridge," said Finn as if he could hardly believe what he was saying.

"The Dunbar Bridge? That's due for a major overhaul. Been off limits for years."

"You're right," said Luke looking at Finn. "But we

made it."

Steve and Don gave Finn and Luke a look of respect.

Within minutes they were hovering over the wreck of the Cessna and the trees the plane had felled. There was no sign of life.

"Don will winch me down," said Steve. "Just how badly injured do you think they are?"

"My father's hurt his leg," replied Luke.

"I don't know what's wrong with my dad," said Finn, looking very worried. "He may have internal injuries. He was in a lot of pain and he couldn't move."

"We'll sort them out," said Steve in an attempt at reassurance, but Luke only felt a deepening despair which he was convinced Finn was sharing. How could they have survived? Wasn't Steve going to find them both dead?

The helicopter hovered above the wreck of the Cessna while Steve was winched down to make his inspection. As they continued to hover, he pulled aside the barricade of branches and clambered through the fuselage.

Steve was inside the wreck for what seemed like an eternity, and the tension rose to such a degree that both Luke and Finn were in an agony of apprehension and could find no words to comfort each other. Despite the noise of the rotors, Luke felt as if he was encapsulated in a terrible silence. As the minutes ticked by, he became convinced that both his father and uncle were dead and glancing round at Finn's agonised expression, Luke guessed that Finn was feeling exactly the same.

Don Parker made no attempt to falsely reassure them, for which Luke was extremely grateful. He was busy relaying information back to Rock, giving location details and reporting the rescue of Finn and Luke. But suddenly Finn began to say, over and over again, "They'll be OK. I'm sure they will."

Luke didn't reply.

Then Steve suddenly emerged from the wreck of the Cessna. For a moment he paused, looking up at the helicopter, and Luke was certain he had found them dead. Then Steve gave a thumbs-up sign and Luke felt a wild rush of elation. He turned to Finn.

"Thank God," he said.

Finn gave him a watery smile and then buried his face in his hands.

When Steve was winched back inside the helicopter he turned to Luke and Finn and said, "They'll both be OK. You're right – your dad's got a fractured leg, but that seems to be about all – apart from a few cuts and bruises." He paused. "As far as Brett's concerned, I think he's got a dislocated shoulder or maybe a broken collarbone."

Finn gasped at this last minute bad news. "What does that mean? Is he going to be—"

"No. It's painful, but not life-threatening. The hospital will have to check him out. They kept quite warm in the sleeping bags and they've even still got some food left. Your father was able to hobble about a bit and look after his brother, he said. We should airlift them back to Rock as soon as we can," said Steve and Don nodded agreement.

"I've radioed for another chopper, and they'll be here in minutes."

"Let me have a look at that ankle of yours." Steve knelt beside Finn and checked him out. After a while he said, "This is nasty and it's gone septic. No wonder you've got a fever. I need to give you an injection right away to tide you over. There's a medical unit back at base where you'll get sorted out properly."

Finn nodded gratefully as the helicopter continued to rise. "I know I've been a fool," he said to Luke when Steve had returned to his seat beside Don.

"You're not a fool." Luke reacted fast. "You had to believe he was alive." He knew Finn was thinking of his delusion about Karl.

"Maybe I did. But our expedition taught me a lot of stuff. Like what to accept and what not. Dad could have died too – but he didn't. Karl's dead though. He's not running with the wolves at all." Finn looked away and Luke knew he had to leave him alone.

They had been through so much together that Luke felt a real bond with his cousin at last. But there wasn't anything he could do for Finn right now. He had to grieve for Karl for the first time.

As the helicopter banked over the mountains in the fading light, Luke saw dark shadows running through the snow. The young wolf was still out in front, running ahead of the pack.

The Great White

"There's a Great White," said Manuel Gonzales. "He's a killer – and I should know." He fingered the shark-tooth necklace round his neck. "I caught one of those devils a couple of years ago and made myself this."

Jack and Carrie watched the fin of the shark travelling through the water behind *Mexican Eagle*, a motor cruiser designed for tourists and owned by Manuel and his brother Juan.

"How big is he?" asked Jack.

"About six metres long," said Manuel. "You can

always recognise the Great White by his torpedo-shaped body and white bony teeth. Then there's that quivering snout with the nostrils trying to scent food."

Jack had never heard him speak such good English. Then he realised he must have mugged it up so that he could shock the tourists.

"Did you really catch a Great White yourself, or are you just making it up?" demanded Jack suspiciously.

Manuel laughed uneasily. "Of course I did," he said and looked away.

Jack couldn't work out whether Manuel was a fake or not.

"Once he smells blood, he's on target," Manuel chuckled, his wide, dark tanned face wreathed in a grin.

"You're just winding us up," said Carrie, Jack's younger sister.

"No, my little one – I'm not winding you up. The Great White's only got two objectives – feeding and breeding. What you can see at the moment is the top fin, slicing through the water like a submarine with its periscope up. Watch – I'll give him a few fish scraps – then you might believe what I'm telling you."

"What else do they eat – besides human beings?" asked Jack.

"The Great White hunts seals and sea lions, dolphins or swordfish. They even eat smaller sharks, but right here they go for elephant seals. Humans are a treat. A rare treat." Manuel grinned again. "But humans are only at risk if they're splashing about, or maybe if they've cut themselves on a rock and there's blood in the water."

Manuel was short and powerfully built. He was in his early thirties and the muscles in his arms stood out like whipcords as he picked up a heavy pail and threw the scraps overboard.

"Watch out for unexpected visitors – one of the sharks could jump right out of the water on to our boat!"

"Thanks for telling us," said Jack drily.

"What's in that pail?" asked Carrie, wrinkling up her nose.

"It's called chum."

"Sounds like dog food."

Manuel gave Carrie a puzzled look. "I'm talking about a mixture of blood and rotting fish."

"Yuk!" was all that Carrie could reply and Jack suddenly felt queasy and hoped he wasn't going to be violently sick. Fortunately the feeling soon disappeared.

"Did you know these sharks are descended from monsters?" asked Manuel with increasing enjoyment. Now Jack was sure he was setting out to wind them all up.

"What kind of monsters?" he asked, watching the chum floating on the surface.

"Prehistoric. The Latin name for the Great White is *Carcharodon Megalodon*." Manuel sounded as if he was reading from his well-worn script again. "That translates as megatooth shark which, I think, is entirely appropriate. Did you know that Carcharodon teeth have been brought up from the ocean floor?"

"No," said Jack.

"And did you know they measure five inches in length and that fossilised teeth of the same size have been found in rocks?"

"No," said Jack again.

Manuel paused for effect and then said, "Watch out for the Great Whites. They're also known as white death."

"Nice one." This time Jack shivered.

Suddenly a huge blunt head with a wide gash of a mouth and a staring black eye on either side of a huge snout burst out of the water. The Great White's teeth were triangular and chunky looking, but Jack was sure they were also razor sharp and there seemed to be dozens of them. As it began to feed on the chum, the shark's eyes rolled back in their sockets, revealing the white surface of its eyeballs. Jack gazed at the thing in horror. Manuel's build-up had been tame beside the grim reality of the shark itself.

But slowly his shock subsided. Jack knew he was well out of its reach, that he was watching it from the deck of *Mexican Eagle*, almost as if he was watching a film. He was safe, protected, in his own world. The shark inhabited another – an ocean that was cruel, mysterious and relatively unexplored. They had no connection with each other. But, all the same, he was relieved when the terrible head disappeared back under the surface with a mouthful of bait.

"Wow," said Dave. "He *was* a big fella."

Manuel grinned, delighted that his sales talk had so convincingly sprung to life.

Jack winced, wishing his stepfather wouldn't be so

embarrassing. He was always saying something uncool.

Jack gazed down at the surface again and saw that the shark must have dived, for there was no trace of him, not even his dorsal fin.

The Simmonds were on holiday in California and had chartered *Mexican Eagle* with another family for a whale-watching trip on the Pacific Ocean. Already Dave Simmonds had got them all laughing uneasily with his corny jokes. He was beginning to get on Jack's nerves and Carrie felt the same.

Their own father had died when Jack was six and Carrie was four. Although he was now twelve and Carrie was ten, the hurt of losing their real father was still just as strong. Dave always seemed to be showing off and trying to get them to love him. But Jack was certain they never would.

Mum had married Dave a few months ago. Both Jack and Carrie knew how lonely she'd been, but if only she'd married someone else!

Dave was showing off even now, trying to impress the Charltons who were also British, and had two young children.

"What's the stomach capacity of a shark?" Dave

asked Manuel. "I bet it's vast." He stood there in his Bermuda shorts, khaki shirt, white socks and sandals, fat and pale-skinned, with carroty hair, his arm round Mum's shoulders as if he owned her. She was willowy and slim and he almost had to stand on tiptoe.

Jack felt hot with embarrassment, sure that Manuel must think his stepfather was a complete fool. But Manuel smiled blandly. He had a business to run and Dave was a customer.

"You're right, Senor," he said. "The Great White's stomach is enormous. Much bigger than mine."

PREDATOR

Are you ready to face White Death?

Read the rest of *Shark Attack*
to find out what happens next!

Can Tom combat Lion Country?

A pride of lions circles its prey. Tom can see the killer instinct in their eyes.
It's one big, adrenalin-fuelled chase. But this is no pumped-up action movie. There's no "pause" button, no "rewind". And Tom must hit the ground running…if he wants to stay alive!

ISBN 1 84121 908 8   £4.99

Got the guts for some Grizzly Action?

A great grizzly zooms into focus. It's the photo opportunity of a lifetime...
if Glen had a camera. And there's another
threat to his safety – the forest fire. Will this
shoot cost Glen his life? Or can he escape
from the deathtrap?

ISBN 1 84121 910 X   £4.99

More Orchard Red Apples

Predator

❑ Shark Attack	Anthony Masters	1 84121 906 1	£4.99
❑ Deathtrap	Anthony Masters	1 84121 910 X	£4.99
❑ Killer Instinct	Anthony Masters	1 84121 908 8	£4.99

Danger

❑ Aftershock!	Tony Bradman	1 84121 552 X	£3.99
❑ Hurricane!	Tony Bradman	1 84121 588 0	£3.99

Jiggy McCue Stories

❑ The Poltergoose	Michael Lawrence	1 86039 836 7	£4.99
❑ The Killer Underpants	Michael Lawrence	1 84121 713 1	£4.99
❑ The Toilet of Doom	Michael Lawrence	1 84121 752 2	£4.99
❑ Maggot Pie	Michael Lawrence	1 84121 756 5	£4.99
❑ The Fire Within	Chris d'Lacey	1 84121 533 3	£4.99
❑ The Salt Pirates of Skegness	Chris d'Lacey	1 84121 539 2	£4.99

Orchard Red Apples are available from all good bookshops,
or can be ordered direct from the publisher:
Orchard Books, PO BOX 29, Douglas IM99 1BQ
Credit card orders please telephone 01624 836000 or fax 01624 837033
or e-mail: bookshop@enterprise.net for details.

To order please quote title, author and ISBN
and your full name and address.
Cheques and postal orders should be made payable to 'Bookpost plc.'
Postage and packing is FREE within the UK
(overseas customers should add £1.00 per book).

Prices and availability are subject to change